LEONTINE BLYTHEWOOD

The Duke's Inherited Bride

Copyright © 2024 by Leontine Blythewood

All rights reserved. No part of this publication may be reproduced, stored or transmitted in any form or by any means, electronic, mechanical, photocopying, recording, scanning, or otherwise without written permission from the publisher. It is illegal to copy this book, post it to a website, or distribute it by any other means without permission.

This novel is entirely a work of fiction. The names, characters and incidents portrayed in it are the work of the author's imagination. Any resemblance to actual persons, living or dead, events or localities is entirely coincidental.

First edition

This book was professionally typeset on Reedsy.
Find out more at reedsy.com

Contents

1	The Funeral	1
2	The Unwanted Crown	5
3	The Inherited Responsibilities	10
4	Bound by Duty, Chained by Doubt	14
5	A Proposal Out of Duty	19
6	A Daughter's Dilemma	23
7	The Bitter Bargain	27
8	The Duchess's Crown	31
9	The Wedding of Necessity	36
10	A Distant Union	40
11	The Ties That Chafe	44
12	Unfamiliar Territory	49
13	Misinterpreted Silence	53
14	In the Shadows of What-If	59
15	The Unwanted Gifts	62
16	The Glimpses of Integrity	66
17	An Unexpected Gesture	70
18	A Necessary Sacrifice	75
19	The Silent Bargain	79
20	A Bitter Obligation	82
21	The Detached Duty	86
22	A Growing Resentment	89
23	More than just Duty	94
24	Unexpected Softness	98
25	The Things I didn't Realize Before	102
26	A New Light	105

27	From Duty to Desire	109
28	A Spark of Betrayal	113
29	A Desperate Rejection	117
30	An Unwanted Confession	121
31	The Unwanted Resilience	127
32	An Uneasy Truce	131
33	The Truth Revealed	135
34	The Apology	140
35	Unspoken Regrets and New Promises	144
36	A Father's Promise	147
37	The Journey Home	151
38	A Storm Brewing	155
39	Facing the Ordeal Together	160
40	The Futile Effort	164
41	The Birth	167
42	A Love Beyond Duty	171
43	Love Refined	175
About the Author		181

1

The Funeral

The rain fell in a fine, cold drizzle as they lowered Simon into the ground, each shovelful of earth muffling what remained of my brother. The sound echoed through me like a bell tolling, the rhythm marking the end of something I could never get back. I stood motionless, a hollow ache spreading through my chest, as heavy as the slate-gray clouds pressing down on us. It felt as though the world had shrunk, collapsing under the weight of Simon's absence. My only family was gone, leaving me alone amidst the responsibilities and expectations that I had never wanted.

Simon was supposed to be the one to bear the title, the duties, and the weight of our family's legacy. He'd always been the one with the charm and wit to navigate the endless responsibilities of being the Duke, while I stood comfortably in the shadows, content to let him shine. But the shadows felt darker now, pressing in from all sides. I clenched my jaw, a desperate effort to hold back the grief that twisted inside me, threatening to break loose. The Harringtons did not cry—not in public, not at funerals. Yet my fingers, wrapped around the small prayer book in my pocket, trembled. The cold, damp leather was the only anchor I had, keeping me from unraveling.

The crowd surrounding me was silent, their eyes respectfully averted. Their presence should have been comforting, but all I felt was how little any of them truly understood. These people had known Simon as the Duke, the bright light in the room with the easy smile, the one everyone turned to for warmth.

To me, he was so much more. He was my brother, my only constant—the person who had shared every joy, every failure, and every painful memory since our childhood. He'd been my safety net, the one who could pull me out of my own darkness, and now he was gone.

I could still picture him, full of life, his laughter echoing through the halls of our estate, his presence filling every room. The notion that he could be reduced to a lifeless body—taken by something so mundane, so tragically ordinary as a fall—felt absurd. Simon, who had always seemed invincible, felled by nothing more than a misplaced stone.

"Earth to earth, ashes to ashes, dust to dust..." The reverend's voice broke through the haze, his solemn words steady, each syllable another hammer blow sealing Simon's fate. It was final now, no matter how I resisted. Simon was gone, and with him went any illusion that I could remain who I had been.

The service moved on, and I forced myself to look up, my gaze drifting over familiar faces blurred by rain and mist. Friends, family—all of them wearing the appropriate mask of grief. Lady Josephine, my cousin, had her eyes lowered, dabbing at them with a lace handkerchief. She'd always admired Simon's charm, but I doubted she'd ever understood him. Few had. And then, beyond the rest of the mourners, I saw her.

Jemima Cavendish stood half-hidden at the edge of the crowd, her face shrouded beneath a dark veil. Simon's fiancée. She looked almost like a ghost, her figure blurred by the drizzle, her posture rigid. I had not spoken to her since the news had broken—I couldn't. I didn't know what to say. Was she grieving for the future they had lost? For the plans they had made? My own grief was a storm, and I couldn't fathom how she must feel, standing alone in its aftermath.

A sharp gust of wind snapped me back to the present. The crowd had started to disperse, quiet murmurs filling the damp air. The reverend stepped beside me, his face creased with a look of practiced sympathy. "Your Grace, my condolences," he said softly. The title struck me like a slap. "Your Grace." It was Simon's title, not mine. I had never wanted it. But now there was no avoiding it—the burden was mine to carry.

I nodded, barely hearing the reverend's words as he moved away. I looked back toward Jemima. She hadn't moved, her dark figure still at the edge of the cemetery, apart from everyone else. She looked lost, and despite my own overwhelming grief, something about her pulled at me. She must have felt my gaze because she turned her head, our eyes meeting across the distance. I hesitated, unsure what I could possibly say to her that might offer any comfort.

Slowly, I crossed the muddy ground toward her. As I drew closer, she lifted her head, and I could see her face through the thin veil—pale, drawn, eyes rimmed red but dry. Her gaze met mine, and for a moment we were connected in our shared loss. There were no words that could bridge the chasm left by Simon's absence, but there was something in the way she held herself—something broken that mirrored the emptiness inside me.

"Lady Cavendish," I said quietly, my voice rough. It felt strange to say her name, as though it should have belonged to Simon's lips and not mine. She inclined her head, her movements stiff and mechanical.

"Your Grace," she replied, her voice barely more than a whisper, almost lost in the sound of the rain. I could hear the effort it took for her to speak, each word a struggle against the weight of her own grief.

"I…" I hesitated, my throat tightening. What could I say that would mean anything at all? "Simon… he would have wanted you here," I managed, the words awkward, clumsy against the backdrop of our loss.

She looked down, her gloved hands clasped tightly in front of her. "Yes," she murmured, though her voice held no conviction. I wanted to tell her that I would make sure she was looked after, that she would always have a place within our family. But the words felt hollow. She'd lost the man she loved. How could I, his shadow, offer her any real comfort?

The silence between us stretched, awkward and painful, until she finally lifted her head, her eyes meeting mine once more. "Thank you, Your Grace," she whispered, her voice strained. She took a step back, her figure beginning to blend into the mist, a dark shape fading into the gray world around us.

I watched her go, feeling a sense of loss that went beyond Simon—as if she, too, was slipping away, another link to the life I had known disappearing before my eyes. I turned back to Simon's grave, the rain still falling, cold and relentless, the freshly turned earth a brutal reminder of the finality of it all.

The Duke of Wellesley. It was a title that had always been Simon's, and now it was mine. The weight of it settled over my shoulders, heavy and unwelcome. I felt the burden of expectation pressing down on me, the weight of my family's legacy now resting solely in my hands. There was no one else. No one but me.

2

The Unwanted Crown

The manor was unbearable in its silence. Each room, each hall echoed with the absence of Simon's voice, his footsteps, his laughter that used to fill even the dreariest corners with something like light. Now, the empty space stretched on, pressing down like an invisible weight, reminding me with every silent second that Simon was truly gone.

I paced the length of the drawing room, barely seeing the heavy furniture, the flickering shadows cast by the firelight. This room had been Simon's favorite—a space where he'd entertained, charmed, and held court, effortlessly commanding the attention of anyone in his presence. But now, the fire burned without purpose, a hollow mimicry of the warmth that Simon himself had once provided.

God, he'd made it all look so easy.

I paused before the grand mantle, leaning my hands against the cold stone. My gaze landed on the polished silver tray by the decanters. I could almost hear Simon's voice urging me to pour a drink, as he had so many times before. "One glass is hardly enough to dull the edges of this life, little brother," he'd say, laughter dancing in his eyes. Simon had been my older brother by only a few years, but he'd always made me feel as if he were a lifetime ahead, always ready to pull me along, like a child in need of guidance.

I poured a glass, the amber liquid catching the light, but the thought of drinking it alone left me hollow. I could practically feel his presence beside me, his amused glance as he toasted some impossible feat he'd accomplished, usually at someone else's expense.

And now all of it was mine. The title, the estate, the responsibilities—and the endless expectations that Simon had somehow carried with infuriating ease. The title of Duke should have come with a manual, I thought bitterly, something to ease the weight of the damn thing pressing down on me now. Yet here I stood, the newly minted Duke of Wellesley, and all I could do was feel the same useless, searing grief that had plagued me since the funeral.

Grief, however, was not something a Duke was permitted to feel. That much, I understood.

I turned my gaze toward the window, where the last gray slivers of daylight were fading, replaced by the mist rolling over the estate. Wellesley Manor loomed out of it like some haunting relic, every stone, every shadow infused with memories I could not bring myself to face. Yet they whispered to me, taunting, until I could barely stand it.

My life was no longer my own. The old life I'd led—the one where I could act as the spare, the overlooked younger brother, free to roam and live in relative obscurity—was now gone. I could feel it slipping from my grasp, replaced by Simon's legacy, Simon's expectations. Hell, even Simon's fiancée.

Lady Jemima Cavendish. The mere thought of her sent a jolt through me—a reminder of yet another role I'd inherited from Simon without any say in the matter.

Since the funeral, she'd kept herself carefully distant, offering only the most polite exchanges, her words devoid of any feeling that might betray her thoughts. But her silence had only sharpened the memory of her veiled figure at the graveside, her head bowed, her posture rigid. There had been something unreadable in her demeanor, a tension I couldn't place. Yet I couldn't deny that she, too, was part of my inheritance. A fiancée left in limbo, a life abruptly altered by Simon's death, now bound to me through the tenuous threads of duty.

"Your Grace?"

The sound of my new title jarred me, pulling me from my thoughts. I turned to find Mrs. Hutchins, the housekeeper, standing at the doorway, her hands clasped. She'd been with the family since I was a boy, and yet even she seemed to struggle with the shift in titles, as if reluctant to replace Simon's name with mine.

"Yes, Mrs. Hutchins?" I asked, my voice sounding rougher than I intended.

"There's supper in the dining room, Your Grace." She hesitated, glancing around the empty room, her expression softening. "If... if you'd like to take it there."

I almost laughed, though the sound would have been bitter. Supper alone in the dining room—a cold, formal affair in a cold, silent house. How fitting. "Thank you, Mrs. Hutchins," I said, giving her a nod.

But she lingered, her brows knitting together in that way she did when something troubled her. "If I may, Your Grace, you look... rather unwell. Perhaps a bit of rest..."

I forced a faint smile. "Rest," I murmured, more to myself than to her. "Yes, I suppose that's what I need."

She nodded, satisfied, and slipped out, leaving me to the quiet once more.

Rest. The word seemed absurd. What I needed was direction, some kind of bearing to hold on to as I stumbled forward. But rest? No, that was the last thing I'd find in this place.

Despite myself, I wandered to the dining room, where the table was set with exacting formality, as if awaiting an honored guest. The flickering candlelight cast long shadows across the empty chairs, stretching down the length of the table. I took my seat at the head, the seat that had been Simon's, and found the room echoing back my silence. Here I was, seated at the center of it all, and yet I had never felt more like an intruder in my own home.

My gaze fell to the empty plate before me, the weight of the evening pressing down until I could hardly breathe. I could picture Simon's lively presence across from me, his easy smile as he regaled me with some story about the estate or the hunt, each tale embellished just enough to make me doubt its truth. I could hear his laughter, warm and effortless, filling the room in a way I knew I never could.

The footman appeared to serve the first course, and I barely tasted it, the flavors as bland as the silence surrounding me. My mind drifted back to

Jemima, to the uncertainty surrounding her future—and my own. I could not fathom what she must think of all this, of me, of the shadow I now wore.

The truth was, I hardly knew her. Simon's fiancée, yes, but beyond the polite exchanges and the occasional glimpse of her at social gatherings, she was as much a mystery to me as the estate was. And now, she was part of the life I was expected to step into, a duty that loomed just as heavy as the title.

My fingers drummed against the table as I sat alone in the cavernous dining room, the reality of my new life pressing in on all sides. Inheritances were supposed to bring power, security, honor. But all I could feel was the crushing weight of everything Simon had left behind.

After a few more bites, I pushed the plate away, appetite gone, and leaned back in the chair, staring at the flickering shadows on the ceiling. The responsibility of the dukedom was already beginning to take shape in my mind—a formidable list of tasks, decisions, and expectations, each one more daunting than the last. And as much as I wanted to honor my brother's memory, a dark thought lingered in the back of my mind.

What if I couldn't live up to it? What if I failed, and this entire legacy slipped through my fingers like the sands of time?

I rose, the scrape of the chair against the floor startling in the silence, and left the dining room. The thought of sleep seemed laughable, but still, I made my way up the stairs, hoping that perhaps exhaustion would dull the ache in my chest.

As I passed the portrait gallery, I paused, my gaze drawn to the painting of Simon at the far end of the hall. There he was, painted with all the vigor and charm he'd carried in life, his eyes bright and confident, his smile a faint challenge to the world. And beneath it, an inscription: "Simon Harrington, Duke of Wellesley."

That title was mine now, but it felt wrong. Inadequate. The man in that portrait would have shouldered this legacy effortlessly, would have laughed in the face of the weight I felt dragging me down. He would have known exactly what to do.

But that man was gone. Only I remained.

"Good night, Simon," I murmured, my voice barely a whisper.

And then I turned and walked away, leaving the shadows and silence to follow me up to bed, the mantle of dukedom resting heavy and unwanted on my shoulders.

3

The Inherited Responsibilities

Becoming Duke of Wellesley felt more like a punishment than an honor. The day was barely halfway through, and I was already drowning in ledgers, letters, and accounts, each one demanding my attention as if the estate itself were conspiring to break me. For the better part of a week, I had been entangled in meetings, discussions, and endless signatures. Simon had handled all of this with ease—at least, that's how he'd made it seem, as if being Duke had been as effortless as breathing.

But now it was my burden to carry, and every decision, every signature felt like a test I was bound to fail. I'd never paid much attention to the estate's workings before. Why would I? It had always been Simon's domain, his responsibility. I had lived comfortably in his shadow, knowing that he was there to shoulder the weight of our family's legacy. Now that he was gone, it felt as if the estate were a beast trying to crush me under its paw.

"Your Grace," Mr. Chalmers, the estate steward, said, pulling me from my thoughts. He had a small mountain of papers tucked under one arm and a pen poised in his other hand. Chalmers had been a faithful servant to our family for nearly two decades, and I suspected he was testing my endurance, perhaps comparing it silently to Simon's. "There are a few matters concerning the Northwood leases that need your decision by next week."

I fought back the urge to pinch the bridge of my nose. The Northwood leases... Simon had renewed them every five years without a second thought, yet somehow I was expected to review and approve them as if they were the foundation of an empire. "I assume the tenants are still content with the current arrangement?"

Chalmers nodded. "For the most part, Your Grace. A few minor adjustments, but nothing significant. However, your signature is still required."

"Of course it is," I muttered, scanning the documents. There was no avoiding it—this was my life now. The smooth rhythm of Simon's old routine, the one he had executed with an ease I envied, now fell upon me, jagged and disjointed. For a man who had lived relatively unburdened, these new responsibilities felt suffocating, as if I were bound to a plow that would grind me down to nothing if I dared resist.

As I continued reviewing the leases, another thought struck me. "Chalmers," I said, glancing up. "Simon always handled these... personally, didn't he?"

"He did," Chalmers replied, with a slight smile that seemed to mask a deeper sympathy. "Though he delegated much of the day-to-day affairs to trusted advisors."

Trusted advisors. I supposed Chalmers counted among them now, though the thought offered little comfort. Simon had always known who to trust, who to turn to for counsel, and I was discovering painfully how few allies I had in navigating this new world. It was as if I was fumbling through a dark room, trying to find the path that Simon had walked so effortlessly.

There was a soft knock at the door, and the butler entered, bowing with impeccable timing. "Your Grace, there is another matter which requires your attention. It concerns... Lady Jemima Cavendish."

My stomach tightened, and I set down my pen. I had anticipated this, yet I had hoped to delay the matter, to handle more pressing concerns first. It seemed, however, that Jemima's situation had now risen to the top of my obligations.

"Yes?" I prompted, keeping my tone steady. "What of Lady Jemima?"

Chalmers cleared his throat and gave a cautious nod. "Her family seeks clarity on the engagement. As Simon's intended, Lady Jemima was to become the next Duchess of Wellesley. Her father, Lord Cavendish, has inquired about the future of their arrangement... or whether a new arrangement will be made."

The implication hit me with the force of a blow, though I knew it had been coming. Jemima was, of course, still part of the picture. Or rather, she was supposed to be. And with Simon gone, that duty—like all the others—now fell to me.

I ran a hand over my jaw, leaning back in the chair. "And what is Lord Cavendish suggesting, precisely?"

Chalmers exchanged a quick glance with the butler before clearing his throat once more. "It has been suggested that you... assume Simon's position. Lady Jemima remains a suitable match and comes from a family of significant influence. The Cavendish family sees no reason why the engagement cannot be honored."

"Honored," I echoed softly, letting the word settle over me. It was absurd, the thought of marrying Simon's fiancée, stepping into yet another aspect of his life. But it was precisely that—the absurdity, the preposterousness of it—that made me realize how little choice I had.

Chalmers continued, "Lady Jemima's family will expect some clarity on the matter soon. It would reflect well on both families, and... from what I understand, Lady Jemima would find little objection." He gave a diplomatic shrug, clearly trying to frame the situation as logically as possible. "After all, Your Grace, it would benefit all parties involved. And the estate would benefit from such an alliance."

I could hardly argue that. Jemima was from one of the wealthiest, most respected families in the country. A marriage to her would bring stability and strengthen the Wellesley name. Yet the idea of asking her, of standing in Simon's place, was almost laughable.

I remembered her at the funeral, standing quietly at the back, her figure barely visible beneath the dark veil. She had been a mystery then, a silent presence. I had no more insight into her thoughts now than I had that day. What did she feel about all of this? Was she, too, mourning a future that would never come to pass? Or was she resigned, like I was, to fulfilling a duty that now felt hollow?

"Your Grace," Chalmers said, breaking into my thoughts. "If I may speak plainly?"

I raised an eyebrow, gesturing for him to continue.

"It is a logical choice," he said, his voice low. "Lady Jemima would make an excellent Duchess, and her family has already expressed their willingness to proceed. With all due respect, Your Grace, you have very little to lose."

"Very little to lose," I repeated, my voice carrying a tinge of bitterness I hadn't meant to reveal. But he was right—at least in part. Simon was gone. My choices were limited, boxed in by duty and legacy.

Chalmers cleared his throat, his face impassive. "With Simon gone, Lady Jemima's future lies in limbo. It would be unkind to prolong her uncertainty."

Unkind. A fine choice of words for something as life-altering as a marriage proposal. But still, it was true. The longer I delayed, the longer she would remain adrift, her future as uncertain as mine. If I had any decency, I would do what was necessary.

My gaze drifted to the fire, where the flames licked quietly against the logs. "I will meet with Lord Cavendish," I said at last, my decision as final as it was reluctant. "We'll discuss... the engagement."

Chalmers nodded, seemingly satisfied. "Very good, Your Grace. I will make the necessary arrangements."

The door closed softly behind him, leaving me alone in the flickering light of the study. The reality of what I had just committed to settled heavily in my chest, but I could not let myself think on it too long. Duty, after all, demanded action, not contemplation. And perhaps, with time, the weight of these choices would begin to feel less like chains.

Yet as I sat there, alone in the shadows, I couldn't shake the feeling that I was merely a shadow of the Duke I was expected to be.

4

Bound by Duty, Chained by Doubt

The quill hovered above the paper, trembling in my hand. Words—such simple words on the page—seemed harder to summon than any decision I'd made thus far. Each sentence I scratched out felt hollow, inadequate, as if my own language betrayed me. What did one say when asking to marry one's own brother's fiancée?

"Lord Cavendish..." I murmured aloud, testing the weight of the words, my voice swallowed by the cavernous silence of the study. A single candle flickered beside me, casting weak, uneven light across the empty room. I'd sat here in the silence for what felt like hours, attempting to compose the letter that would cement my fate—and Jemima's—forever.

I dipped the quill in ink, and my hand shook slightly, as if the very act of writing it forced me to acknowledge how far I'd been thrust into Simon's life, even after his death. I would be reaching out to Lord Cavendish with a proposal, a marriage proposal, yet I felt as though I were drafting a death sentence. Not for me, not really. But for the part of me that had once thought I could carve out my own future, beyond the shadows of the dukedom, of Simon, of the expectations that had choked us both from birth.

I paused, the quill hovering again, ink pooling at the tip. How many times had I wished for freedom? For the chance to live my life without the weight of titles and responsibilities? Yet here I was, about to give up even the faintest hope of that. The estate needed this marriage, I reminded myself. Duty demanded it. And yet, the words would not come easily. They were stuck behind the wall of resentment that had grown thicker since Simon's death, each word forced from me as if in penance for daring to want something different.

Lord Cavendish, I wrote at last, the letters blotting as the ink pooled. I sat back, my thoughts catching. In these short days, I had been crushed by the sheer weight of the title, the relentless demands of the estate, and the hollow emptiness Simon's death had left in its wake. I'd barely had time to take in a breath before the expectation of my marriage to Jemima had wrapped around me like a tightening vice. It had been days since I'd known peace.

The mere thought of Jemima, of the life we would be forced into together, unsettled me in a way I couldn't explain. She had been Simon's; the world had known her as his intended. She'd loved him—at least, I assumed she had. I'd watched them, on occasion, during gatherings or dinners, the way they would lean in toward each other, the way her laughter would bloom in response to his easy charm. In the shadows, I'd sometimes found myself envying them, envying the simplicity of their union.

Now, that ease and simplicity were gone. Jemima would come to me reluctantly, I knew. I could still see her at the funeral, her face hidden behind that dark veil, her posture more resigned than grieving, a touch of coldness about her that seemed more suited to the hard stones of the cemetery than to her usual, vibrant self. What must she think of all this? Was she, too, mourning not only Simon but the future that had died with him? Was she resigned to this new, forced path, just as I was?

I tried again, forcing myself to continue the letter.

Lord Cavendish,

It is with the utmost respect that I write to you, hoping to clarify a matter of great importance to both our families. In light of my brother Simon's passing, I have come to realize the pressing nature of Lady Jemima's future—a future that my brother had intended to secure through marriage. I recognize that, as Duke, I now bear the responsibility to fulfill that intention.

The ink blotched slightly as I hesitated, the words sounding both distant and formal, as if they had been spoken by someone else entirely. But what other words could I choose? What other way was there to frame a union that was as inevitable as it was unwanted?

I considered for a brief, irrational moment putting down the quill and abandoning this task altogether. But I had been born and raised for duty, if nothing else. There was no escaping it. My whole life, I'd stood in Simon's shadow, watching as he filled every role, every responsibility with a confidence that had been as effortless as it was infuriating. And now, in his absence, I was to step into his shoes fully, even if they left me crippled.

The estate needed this match. Jemima's family expected it, and though I'd not heard a word from her, I imagined Jemima herself must feel as bound by this duty as I did.

I am prepared to extend my hand in marriage to Lady Jemima, should you and she find this arrangement agreeable.

The words sat there, solid as stone, taunting me. There was no turning back now.

I forced myself to continue, though the words burned with each stroke of the quill.

It is my hope that through this union, we might uphold the alliance our families sought to create, and honor the memory of my brother Simon.

My hand stopped, mid-sentence, the thought freezing me. Honor Simon. The words hung in my mind, twisting into something sharp, something bitter. What honor was there in this? What would Simon have thought, if he were still here, to see me writing this letter, standing in his place, speaking the vows he would have spoken?

Perhaps he would have laughed. Yes, that's how I imagined it. Simon, with his easy smile, would have laughed, clapped me on the shoulder, told me that duty was for the strong-willed. I could almost hear him saying it, see the gleam in his eye, as though none of this would trouble him, as though the weight of it would have slid from his shoulders like water.

And now I, the man who had never wanted any part of this, was writing a letter to make myself his replacement.

I signed the letter with a steady hand, sealing my words in the blackest wax I could find. When it was done, I sat back, the silence of the room settling like a shroud around me. The decision was made. The proposal would be delivered. And soon, Jemima would know.

The thought of her reaction lingered, chilling me. I had no idea how she would respond—if she would welcome the match, if she would even consider it, or if she would turn away from me in scorn. I'd never been able to read her; she had always held herself slightly apart, even in company, as if guarding some inner world that no one could touch. That world had been for Simon, not for me.

And now I was expected to inherit that, too.

The door creaked, and I looked up to see Chalmers, his face drawn, his eyes as watchful as ever. He took one look at the letter, the black wax glistening, and nodded. "It is ready, Your Grace?"

"Yes," I replied, the word sounding hollow. "Please see that it's delivered to Lord Cavendish immediately."

Chalmers took the letter, his expression unreadable. But as he turned to leave, he paused, glancing back at me with a look of something close to pity. "Your Grace," he began, his voice hesitant, "Lady Jemima... she may find comfort in the honor you seek to offer her."

I nodded, not trusting myself to speak. Comfort. The word felt foreign, unfathomable. What comfort could there be for a woman forced into marriage with her dead fiancé's brother? But perhaps that was all we had left— fragments of honor, pieces of duty, cobbled together to form the life we were both bound to lead.

As Chalmers left, closing the door softly behind him, I felt the silence swell, the air thick and heavy. I glanced back down at the empty spot where the letter had been, an ache settling deep in my chest. This was the path before me—the life I'd inherited, not chosen.

But if honor and duty demanded it, then I would do it. For Simon. For Jemima. For the name I bore. Even if it meant losing myself to it entirely.

The candle flickered, casting long shadows that stretched across the study, mirroring the weight that had settled within me. I stood, closing my eyes, letting the darkness rise and fall with my breath.

Tomorrow, I would meet Jemima's father. And in that meeting, my fate—

and hers—would be sealed.

5

A Proposal Out of Duty

Lord Cavendish accepted my offer with a fervor that left me speechless. Not a hint of hesitation in his reply, not a glimmer of reluctance over seeing me, Simon's shadow, in his future son-in-law's place. He thanked me as if I'd done his family a great service, as if I'd gallantly stepped forward to spare his daughter some terrible misfortune. In his response, he insisted that Jemima would receive me "as graciously as possible." Whether he meant it or simply hoped for it, I couldn't tell. His words echoed in my mind, and I felt a pang of guilt and uncertainty. What kind of future was I really offering Jemima? A substitute for the man she had loved, a man who had been everything I was not—charming, confident, effortlessly capable.

And now, with the hour upon me, I was more nervous than I'd been in a lifetime. My stomach twisted with an unfamiliar dread, the kind that made my heart race and my hands tremble. The drawing room was dim, filled with the scent of roses—a soft, quiet fragrance that belied the tension simmering beneath. I straightened, my hands betraying me with a slight tremor as I waited for Jemima to enter. This proposal was to be made formally, properly, with all the ceremony the situation demanded, and yet I felt hollow, going through the motions as if I were only a spectator to my own fate.

The door opened, and she stepped in, her posture rigid. She seemed to float into the room rather than walk, each step carrying an air of grace that felt painfully familiar. She had always been composed, dignified—a woman well-suited to the role of duchess. But there was a distance to her now, something cold that I hadn't seen before, and I found myself wondering if she was as numb to all of this as I was.

"Lady Cavendish." I inclined my head, managing a faint smile, though I doubted it reached my eyes.

"Your Grace." Her voice was even, polite, a veneer as flawless as her poise. She kept her hands clasped before her, and when she lifted her head to meet my gaze, her expression was unreadable. I was left grasping for words, a clumsy feeling for a man supposed to be a Duke, a man who was supposed to lead with confidence.

"Thank you... for meeting me," I said, struggling to sound formal. How strange that these words felt like foreign objects on my tongue, as if I'd rehearsed them a thousand times but still couldn't make them my own. My throat felt tight, and the silence that followed seemed to stretch into eternity, heavy and suffocating.

She inclined her head but said nothing, the silence stretching between us until I felt the weight of it pressing down. I forced myself to continue, each word slow, heavy, laced with guilt.

"You know why I am here." I cleared my throat, struggling to keep my voice steady. "After... after Simon's passing, it became clear that my duty must be to uphold his intentions. Your family and mine have long anticipated a union, and I... I am here to honor that arrangement."

Her hands tightened slightly, her fingers curling around each other, but she gave no other indication of her feelings. "Of course, Your Grace," she replied, her tone impeccably calm. There was a bitterness in it, though—subtle but unmistakable. It stung, the quiet resentment in her voice, though I knew I had no right to expect anything else.

I forced myself to look her in the eye, finding a steely resolve beneath her eyes. I knew then that she would accept this proposal because duty demanded it, just as duty had demanded it of me. But what I hadn't known— what I hadn't been prepared for—was the resentment in her gaze, a quiet fire smoldering just beneath the surface. She was here because she had no other choice, just as I had none. We were both prisoners of duty, bound by expectations neither of us had asked for.

I took a breath, steeling myself. "Lady Cavendish..., I cannot undo what fate has dealt us. But I assure you, I am committed to fulfilling this role as faithfully as Simon would have. I will honor you as my wife, and I will do my utmost to ensure that you want for nothing."

Her mouth twitched, but she made no reply, her silence sharp enough to draw blood. The air between us felt thick, as if we were both trapped beneath a weight we couldn't see, a weight that neither of us could lift alone. I searched her face for something—anything—that might tell me what she was thinking, what she was feeling, but there was nothing. Only that same cold composure, that same distance that seemed to stretch between us like an unbridgeable chasm.

"You must know," I continued, feeling the need to offer something—anything—that might soften this impossible situation, "that this is not something I take lightly. I understand what this costs you. I understand that you had a different life in mind, and I..." I faltered, not knowing how to finish. How could I possibly understand? I was here, asking her to marry me, to step into a life neither of us wanted, and all I had to offer her were empty words, hollow assurances that I knew could never be enough.

"You understand?" she repeated, her voice barely above a whisper. She finally met my gaze, her eyes were dark, turbulent with an emotion I couldn't decipher. "Forgive me, Your Grace, but I don't think you do."

Her words cut through me, the soft scorn in her voice slicing deeper than I could have anticipated. I felt a surge of helplessness, the inadequacy of my own intentions made painfully clear. How could I possibly understand? I was here, offering her what was left of a shattered promise, and all I had were empty assurances, words that rang hollow even to my own ears.

"I am sorry," I said, the apology tumbling out before I could stop it. I hadn't meant to say it, hadn't meant to expose the raw truth beneath my veneer of duty. But there it was, bare and unrefined.

She watched me, her expression softening, if only slightly. But then she looked away, her gaze fixed somewhere beyond me, somewhere I could not reach. "You don't need to apologize, Your Grace," she said quietly. " If this is what must be done then I will do it. I will honor the commitment our families expect of us."

Her words, however graciously spoken, felt like a sentence handed down. She was accepting my proposal not out of love, not even out of duty to me, but out of obligation—a hollow echo of the life she'd once anticipated with Simon. The realization settled in my chest like a stone, heavy and cold, and I found myself wishing, just for a moment, that things could have been different— that we could have been different.

I wanted to say more, to offer her something that might ease the resentment in her voice, but the words died in my throat. She had accepted. That was all that mattered.

Slowly, I reached out, taking her hand. She did not pull away, but she did not clasp my hand in return. Her fingers were cool, unyielding, a silent reminder of the distance that would remain between us. I gave her hand a gentle squeeze, a gesture I hoped might convey some fragment of reassurance, even if she couldn't—or wouldn't—accept it.

"Then it is settled," I said softly, more to myself than to her. "We will be married."

Jemima nodded, her gaze still fixed somewhere beyond me, her voice barely a whisper. "Yes, Your Grace."

I released her hand, feeling the loss of warmth, small as it was. She turned to leave, each step measured, precise, her posture as rigid as ever. She didn't look back, and I was left standing in the dim room, my hand empty, my heart hollow.

As the door closed behind her, the weight of my own words sank in, chilling me to the core.

"Yes," I murmured to the silence, feeling the truth of it settle like a stone in my chest. "It is settled."

Yet, somehow, it felt like nothing was settled at all.

6

A Daughter's Dilemma

I'd expected to feel numb by now. To feel something akin to peace after everything had gone silent, like the deadened calm of a storm once it has finished its ruin.

But as I left the drawing room, the coldness of Josiah's proposal settled within me like stones in my stomach. I could still hear his words echoing in my mind: *"I will do my utmost to ensure that you want for nothing."* Promises that he'd fulfill his duty, that he would honor me as his wife. But that was all he'd offered—nothing more, nothing less. The only commitment binding us was duty, a feeble rope that barely held together the fractured pieces of my life.

Duty. It was a word that seemed so grand from afar but became hollow when tied to one's own fate.

My mind drifted back to Simon, to the last time I'd seen him before he left for that fateful ride. We'd been standing in the garden, the spring sun casting a warm glow over the roses. Simon had leaned casually against a wrought-iron bench, his hat tipped back, his eyes bright and alive. I could hear his laugh as clearly as if he were beside me now, teasing me over some minor disagreement, his voice carrying that unmistakable charm that could turn even the most trivial exchange into something grand and thrilling.

He'd pulled me close, his gloved hand lingering at my waist, his gaze warm and full of promise. "When we're wed, Jemima," he'd whispered, his lips so close to mine, "I'll show you the world, not just as a Duchess but as my companion in every sense. This life will be ours, my dear. Just wait and see."

The memory was so vivid, so alive, that for a moment I felt the ache of his absence more sharply than I had in weeks. I could almost feel his fingers at my waist, that look in his eye that promised endless adventures. He'd made everything feel light, possible—so easy to believe.

Yet here I was, standing alone in a cold hallway, those promises as empty as the air around me. Simon was gone, and in his place stood Josiah—silent, stiff, a man made of formality and restraint. Where Simon had been light, Josiah was shadow; where Simon had been warmth, Josiah was a steady, unyielding coldness. And now, by fate's twisted hand, I was bound to him. My life would be spent beside a man who seemed more a ghost than the brother he'd left behind.

I felt the resentment stir, rising like a bitter tide. Why had it been Simon? Why had Josiah been spared, the quiet, dutiful brother who seemed to carry the world's weight without so much as a glimmer of joy? Simon had been full of life, of laughter, and somehow, cruelly, he had been the one to go.

My thoughts turned to Josiah's proposal, the tightness in his voice when he'd said, *"This is not something I take lightly."* He'd spoken as though the mere idea of marriage to me was a burden he could scarcely bear, as though his honor was all he could offer, not a shred more. The words had been polished, respectful, but beneath them, I had felt the weight of obligation—the sense that he had inherited me just as he had inherited his brother's title and lands.

Inherited. The word made my stomach churn. I'd always known what my place in the world would be; I'd been raised for this role, groomed to be a duchess. But I'd imagined that Simon and I would take it on together, that we would make this life ours. In those final moments in the garden, I'd felt like the future was something we'd crafted between us—a future full of joy and light, with him by my side.

I could still see him turning to wave at me, that charming, crooked grin lighting his face before he mounted his horse. I'd never thought it would be the last time I would see him alive, never thought that his laugh would haunt me in this cold, empty house. The memory of that day replayed in my mind like a cruel refrain, a reminder of what could have been—and what would never be.

I took a deep, unsteady breath, letting my hand fall to my side. This wasn't the life I'd chosen. I was to marry Simon, the man I'd loved, the man who'd promised me a future worth living. And now I was to be given to Josiah, a man who saw me only as a duty to fulfill. The resentment grew sharper, cutting through me like glass, leaving me raw and exposed.

A soft voice broke the silence, startling me from my thoughts. "Lady Jemima?"

It was my maid, Sarah, her expression cautious, as though she could sense the turmoil simmering beneath my composure. "Shall I prepare your things for this evening?"

I managed a nod, my throat tightening. "Yes, thank you, Sarah." The words felt forced, stiff, as if I were wearing a mask that didn't quite fit.

She lingered for a moment, her brow furrowing, then dropped her gaze respectfully before disappearing down the hall.

As her footsteps faded, I found myself moving to the window, my gaze drifting over the gray expanse of the grounds. This was to be my home, my life. And the man I would share it with… he was little more than a stranger to me, bound by nothing but obligation and our mutual grief. I wanted to hate him, wanted to find a reason to let this resentment grow until it swallowed any possibility of warmth or understanding.

But even in my bitterness, I couldn't entirely blame him. Josiah had not asked for this any more than I had. He, too, had been thrust into a role he hadn't chosen, saddled with responsibilities that weren't his by nature or desire. I'd seen the tension in his eyes, the hesitation that betrayed his own reluctance. And yet, despite that, he'd offered me whatever scraps of honor he had, his voice taut with the weight of his promise.

I closed my eyes, letting the memory of Simon fade, though it left me feeling emptier than before. Duty. Honor. These words meant little to me now, shadows of ideals that felt hollow when forced into reality. But they were all I had left, the last remnants of a future I'd lost.

If Josiah was willing to endure this arrangement for the sake of family, of obligation, then I could do no less. Perhaps, in time, we might find a semblance of peace. Perhaps the bitterness would fade, and we would settle into a life that was at least bearable.

But even as I told myself this, I felt the sorrow deepen, the ache of knowing that all of this—the title, the promise, the future—had been meant for another man. A man I had loved, and who had loved me, or so I'd thought. The life I'd envisioned was gone, replaced by something colder, something forced, and yet... it was my only option.

With one last look at the bleak sky outside, I straightened, smoothing down my skirts. Whatever lay ahead, I would meet it with the same grace that had carried me this far. And if my heart ached, if my spirit rebelled, no one would know. Not even Josiah.

Turning from the window, I steeled myself. Tonight, I would be the dutiful daughter, the dutiful fiancée. Tonight, I would face Josiah again, prepared to meet this fate head-on, no matter how bitterly it tasted.

And perhaps, in time, I might even convince myself that this life—this shadow of the one I'd dreamed—was enough.

7

The Bitter Bargain

The evening air was thick with the low hum of voices, a steady undercurrent of polite conversation echoing through the drawing room. The fire crackled in the hearth, casting a warm glow over the polished wood and gilded frames that lined the walls, but the room felt colder to me than ever. My mother had arranged a quiet, formal dinner, a customary gathering in advance of our engagement to allow both families the opportunity to affirm what was now inevitable. My stomach knotted as I took my seat, fighting to maintain a composed expression, even as resentment simmered beneath the surface.

Josiah entered shortly after I did, his steps measured, his expression as stoic as ever. I watched him take his place at the opposite end of the table, a study in formality and restraint. He offered me a polite nod, his gaze lingering on me just long enough to be respectful but never lingering. The air between us felt strained, as though we were two actors forced to play roles neither of us wanted.

I couldn't help but compare him to Simon, my mind drifting back to the last dinner we had shared before his death. I could still remember the way he'd leaned toward me, his eyes bright with mischief as he whispered some jest that was just risqué enough to make me blush but not scandalous enough to raise my mother's suspicions. He had made everything feel like a shared adventure, even the tedious traditions that I'd so often resented. Simon had a way of filling any room with his warmth, his laugh a balm that could ease even the most stifling formalities.

But Josiah... Josiah was a different sort of man entirely. He sat upright, his shoulders tense, his face a mask of propriety. His eyes held none of Simon's easy charm, none of that infectious sparkle. Where Simon had seemed to fill every corner of the room with his presence, Josiah seemed determined to fade into it, his demeanor so restrained it bordered on icy.

My parents took their seats, my mother settling beside me with a faint, contented smile as she surveyed the scene. My father, ever the picture of authority, nodded approvingly toward Josiah, clearly satisfied with the match. "Well," he began, his voice carrying a note of finality, "it is a comfort to know that both of you are committed to fulfilling the legacy Simon left behind."

I felt my heart clench, a pang of loss mingling with frustration. A legacy. That was what Simon had been reduced to—a title, a duty, an obligation to be passed from one brother to the next. And here I was, no longer a beloved fiancée but an asset, something that had to be secured, signed, and sealed. I swallowed, my gaze shifting to Josiah, who sat still as stone, his expression betraying no hint of his own feelings on the matter.

"So," my father continued, looking at Josiah with approval, "do you have any thoughts on when you might wish to proceed with the arrangements?"

Josiah's jaw tightened almost imperceptibly, his hand resting on the table with a measured stillness that spoke volumes. "Whenever Lady Jemima feels ready, of course," he replied, his tone respectful but distant. His eyes flickered to me briefly before lowering again, as if the mere act of looking at me too long would reveal something he was determined to keep hidden.

I forced a smile, nodding in silent agreement, though the very thought of moving forward filled me with dread. Beside me, my mother's hand rested lightly on mine, her eyes brimming with pride as she gave a slight, approving squeeze. I was expected to accept this marriage, this life, with grace and obedience. I was expected to be the dutiful daughter, to fulfill my role without question.

But as I sat across from Josiah, I couldn't shake the gnawing sense of loss. I hadn't expected to love Simon when our engagement was first arranged—it had been a matter of duty, a match that would unite our families, nothing more. And yet Simon had surprised me. He'd turned our engagement into something real, something filled with warmth and hope. He'd given me a glimpse of a future that I'd never dared to imagine—a life that felt like mine, shaped by laughter and companionship.

I looked across the table at Josiah, my gaze lingering on his features, sharp and unmoving as if he were carved from stone. His silence, his restraint, his relentless adherence to formality—all of it felt like a wall, a barrier that kept him unreachable. How was I supposed to spend a lifetime with a man who seemed to hold his very soul under lock and key?

When Simon had spoken of our future, his words had been laced with promises of joy, companionship, and adventure. But Josiah's words—the ones he'd uttered when he proposed—echoed in my mind, hollow and unfeeling. *"I will do my utmost to ensure that you want for nothing."* Not a word more, not a hint of warmth or affection. Only duty. The very thing that held me here, that bound us both, a shackle that had more weight than any vow.

I felt a surge of resentment, my hands curling into fists beneath the table. How could fate be so cruel, so arbitrary? How could it take from me the one person who had promised me a life of happiness, only to leave me with this—a man who seemed as distant as the moon, a stranger bound to me by little more than a sense of obligation?

As the dinner continued, I felt my mind drifting, my thoughts slipping further and further away from the formalities. Josiah's voice reached me in fragments, polite responses to my father's questions, each one precise and measured, as if he were reciting lines from a well-rehearsed script.

"My dear," my father's voice broke through my thoughts, pulling me back to the present. "Do you have any thoughts on the matter?"

I looked up, startled, realizing with embarrassment that I had missed the last several exchanges. "Oh, yes... of course," I stammered, my cheeks flushing as I struggled to recall the topic at hand. "I... I defer to Lord Harrington's judgment," I said, my voice sounding strange to my own ears, distant and hollow.

Josiah's eyes met mine for the briefest of moments, a flicker of something passing over his face before his expression returned to its customary restraint. I wondered if he felt it too—the weight of this arrangement, the emptiness that lingered between us, filled only by the ghost of what might have been. But as quickly as the thought appeared, I dismissed it. Josiah, as far as I could tell, was utterly unbothered by the nature of our union. For him, it was simply a matter of duty, nothing more.

The evening dragged on, a series of stilted exchanges and forced smiles. I could feel the edges of my composure fraying, the strain of pretending weighing on me with each passing minute. Finally, as the last course was cleared away, my mother rose, signaling that it was time to bring the evening to a close.

Josiah stood, bowing politely as he took his leave, his gaze barely brushing mine as he moved toward the door. I watched him go, feeling a pang of something I couldn't quite name—a strange blend of resentment and longing, a sense of loss for something that had never even had the chance to exist.

As the door closed behind him, I let out a shaky breath, the weight of the evening pressing down on me like a stone. This was my future—a life bound to a man I barely knew, a man who seemed incapable of warmth or passion. I'd thought I could bear it, that I could carry the mantle of duty as I'd been taught. But as I stood there, alone in the silence, I felt a hollow ache settle within me, a quiet despair that whispered of the life I'd lost and the shadows that had taken its place.

With one last look at the empty room, I turned and made my way upstairs, each step echoing in the quiet. Tonight, I would be the dutiful daughter, the dutiful fiancée. But as I reached my room, closing the door behind me, I allowed myself the luxury of a single tear, a silent acknowledgment of the life that would never be.

And though I swore I would bury that bitterness deep within me, as I lay in bed that night, I knew that the ache would remain, a quiet, unyielding reminder of what had been stolen from me and the cold, empty future that now lay ahead.

8

The Duchess's Crown

I could feel the pins pressing into my scalp, each twist and pull securing my hair into a style so intricate it might as well have been armor. My mother's hands moved quickly, each tug precise, as if somehow, with every pin, she could stitch my crumbling world back together. But the chill in my chest remained, untouched by all her primping and fussing. No amount of grooming could change what was happening, or how very little choice I had in it.

My mother's eyes flickered to mine in the reflection, a small frown pulling at the corners of her mouth. "Jemima, dear, it would help if you smiled," she said, smoothing a lock of my hair that had already been twisted into place. "A Duchess ought to look radiant, not..." She let the words hang, and I knew she wanted to say melancholy, or perhaps haunted, but was too polite to speak it aloud.

I forced my lips into what I hoped resembled a smile, though it felt more like a grimace. She had no patience for anything but grace on this day. And why would she? To her, this arrangement was perfection itself, a second chance at a future that had seemed all but lost the day Simon died.

"Mother," I whispered, my voice barely more than a breath. "Must I go through with this?"

Her hands paused mid-motion, and for a fleeting moment, I thought I saw something soft in her gaze, a flicker of compassion or understanding. But just as quickly, her expression hardened, and she straightened, smoothing the front of her own gown with a sharp tug.

"Jemima, it is only sensible," she replied, her tone brisk, as though she were speaking of arranging flowers rather than my entire life. "This marriage is what's best for you. It will restore the future that Simon's death nearly robbed from us. You should be grateful that Josiah is willing to fulfill this duty."

Grateful. The word twisted in my stomach, sharp and bitter. She made it sound as though Josiah had made some great sacrifice, when in reality he was as trapped by duty as I was. Perhaps that was what made it so painful—knowing that neither of us wanted this, yet we were forced to play our parts as if it were all a grand performance.

My mother's hands resumed their task, straightening the lace at my collar, smoothing the fabric of my dress. "Besides," she continued, her tone softening slightly, "there is no greater blessing than to be a Duchess. You will want for nothing, Jemima. The Wellesleys are one of the oldest, most respected families in the country. This is the life every woman dreams of."

"Not every woman," I murmured under my breath, though I knew better than to say it aloud.

To her, this marriage was not only acceptable but ideal. A Duchess's title, the security of a powerful family, a life that, from the outside, seemed to glitter. To her, I was being saved from a bleak, uncertain future. But to me, it felt like shackles, binding me to a life with a man I neither loved nor trusted. A man I barely even knew, whose reputation whispered through the halls like a dark shadow.

There were rumors—whispers that Josiah was not as steadfast as he appeared. Some said he had a lover hidden away, others that he even had an illegitimate child. When I had voiced my concerns to my mother, her response had been dismissive, her expression sharp. "Jemima, you need only bear a legitimate heir for Josiah," she had said, her voice as cold as the steel pins in her hands. "After that, any illegitimate child or sordid rumor will no longer matter. You will be Duchess, and that is all anyone will care about."

Her words had settled in my chest like a stone, heavy and unmoving. It was as though my entire worth was reduced to my ability to produce an heir, to secure the lineage of the Wellesleys. Love, affection, trust—none of it mattered in her eyes, nor in the eyes of the society we lived in. My role was clear, my purpose defined, and there was no room for sentimentality.

"Don't you see?" My mother's voice softened, and her eyes met mine with something close to affection, even pride. "This is your chance to rise above the sorrow of Simon's loss. You will have a life of stability, respect, and admiration. You will be the mistress of Wellesley Manor, with every comfort at your fingertips. What could be better?"

"Simon," I replied, barely audible, the word slipping out before I could stop it. The name hung in the air between us, a ghostly reminder of what had been lost and what could never be reclaimed.

She sighed, her expression a mixture of impatience and pity. "Darling, Simon is gone. There is no sense in dwelling on it. He would want you to be happy, to move forward. Do you not think he would have chosen the same for you, if he could?"

I swallowed hard, my throat tight, the ache of Simon's absence throbbing anew. How easy it was for her to say these things, as if the love I had shared with him could be easily transferred to his brother, as though marriage were a transaction, a calculated arrangement. Perhaps, to her, it was.

But to me, the thought of standing beside Josiah, of facing a lifetime of duty without warmth or affection... It felt like a sentence rather than a blessing. And the rumors, the whispers of his indiscretions, only made it worse. How could I trust a man who carried the shadow of such scandal, who might already have a child born out of wedlock? How could I find peace in a marriage that seemed destined to be haunted by secrets?

Yet, even as I stood there, wreathed in lace and silk, my heart heavy with despair, I knew there was no escape. The decision had been made for me the moment Simon died. My father had accepted Josiah's proposal without hesitation, relieved to have the matter resolved so neatly. To him, it was a practical choice, a way to salvage what remained of the future he'd envisioned for me. The future he'd never bothered to ask if I wanted.

Unless I ran away or died, this marriage would happen.

The thought flitted through my mind, as dark as it was brief. I imagined myself slipping away, disappearing into some far corner of the world where no one knew my name, where I could shed the weight of expectations and live on my own terms. But even as the thought crossed my mind, I knew it was impossible. I would not—could not—do that to my family, to my mother and father, whose dreams for me had always revolved around this life, this marriage.

With a final tug, my mother stepped back, surveying me with satisfaction. "There," she said, her smile proud and expectant. "Now, let's see that smile again, Jemima."

I forced my lips into a semblance of a smile, the kind that might satisfy her, but the effort left me weary, hollow. I could feel the sheen of tears prickling at the edges of my vision, but I blinked them back, refusing to let them fall. Crying would solve nothing, and showing weakness now would only fuel her disappointment.

The door opened, and my father entered, his eyes scanning me with approval, his expression pleased. "You look lovely, my dear," he said, his tone warm, as if he were speaking to a cherished possession rather than his only daughter. "The Wellesleys will be proud to have you as their Duchess."

I nodded, the weight of his words settling over me like a shroud. The Wellesleys. Not even Josiah himself, but the family, the name, the legacy. It was as if I were marrying into an institution rather than a partnership, as if my purpose was to serve a title rather than to live a life.

But I had no choice. My fate was sealed, my path set before me, and there was nothing I could do to change it. My mother had already begun to fuss with my veil, adjusting it until it hung perfectly, shrouding my face in delicate lace, the final layer of armor that would hide the truth from everyone who looked at me.

She pressed a kiss to my cheek, her eyes bright with excitement, and for a moment, I wondered if she truly believed that this was a happy day, a day worth celebrating. Perhaps, in her world, it was.

But in mine, it felt like the end of something precious, something that could never be reclaimed.

I squared my shoulders, breathing in deeply, willing myself to stay composed. Today, I would walk forward, step by step, into the life that had been chosen for me. Today, I would become Lady Jemima Harrington, Duchess of Wellesley, with all the poise and grace my family demanded.

And perhaps, one day, I would convince myself that it was enough.

9

The Wedding of Necessity

The day dawned shrouded in an uneasy stillness. The light filtered through a haze of mist, casting an almost ghostly pall over Wellesley Manor, as if the very air sensed the unnaturalness of what was to take place. I'd dressed in silence, every movement heavy with the weight of the day. Duty. Honor. Responsibility. The words were becoming a chant, hollow mantras I repeated to myself as if they could lessen the unease churning in my gut.

It should have been Simon standing here today. He would have laughed, perhaps whispered something entirely improper in Jemima's ear, something that would have made her smile, even laugh. But as I stood waiting at the altar, I was acutely aware of my own silence, my own inability to fill that role. I couldn't be Simon, and that was precisely the problem. The absence of his laughter, his ease, his warmth left a void that I was helpless to fill, and I felt the weight of it pressing on my chest like a heavy stone.

The ceremony itself was more spectacle than I'd imagined—rows of esteemed guests, all finely dressed, gathered like solemn statues on either side of the chapel. Some glanced at me with a vague curiosity, others with pity, as if they knew, as I did, that this was not the life I would have chosen. But it was the life I had, and so I stood, spine straight, jaw clenched, forcing myself to play the part. I tried to focus on my breathing, to still the racing thoughts that ran circles in my mind, but the tension in my shoulders only seemed to grow.

And then the doors opened, and she appeared.

Jemima moved down the aisle with a grace that looked effortless, her gown a cascade of white lace and silk that caught the light. Her face was hidden behind a delicate veil, but I could see the stiffness in her posture, the tightness in her shoulders. She walked toward me like a woman stepping into battle, every inch of her controlled and unyielding. It broke my heart in a way I couldn't explain, knowing that she was stepping into this with the same sense of resignation I felt.

Her father escorted her, his expression proud, his gaze fixed ahead. I could feel his satisfaction from across the room, his approval of this union that would keep the Cavendish name bound to a powerful family. He handed Jemima's gloved hand to mine without hesitation, as if transferring ownership, and I felt the faintest tremor in her fingers before she stilled, withdrawing any hint of warmth. Her hand felt fragile in mine, and I wished, just for a moment, that I could offer her something—anything—to ease her fear.

She looked up, and our eyes met for the first time that day. Behind the thin lace of her veil, her gaze was dark, searching, filled with something sharp and unreadable. Suspicion, perhaps. Or disdain. I couldn't be certain, but I sensed that she was watching me closely, as if she expected some hidden motive, some cruel twist of fate lurking behind this arrangement. I held her gaze, trying to convey some sense of reassurance, but her expression remained guarded, as though every word I'd spoken to her until now had been a deception.

I wanted to say something, anything that might ease the tension between us, but the solemnity of the moment held me captive. Words would be pointless, anyway. She wasn't looking for comfort; she was looking for answers to questions I didn't know how to answer. How could I, when I was as uncertain as she was?

The vicar began the ceremony, his voice low and reverent, reciting each vow with practiced cadence. I repeated the words, the promises that bound us, though they felt foreign, as if I were saying them on behalf of someone else. I glanced at Jemima, but she kept her gaze averted, her profile set in cold detachment. I could see the tension in the line of her jaw, the way her lips pressed into a thin, unyielding line.

As the vicar instructed her to repeat her vows, Jemima's voice was steady, controlled. Each word fell like a carefully measured stone, void of the warmth or joy one might expect on such a day. She spoke them as if they were a sentence handed down, final and inescapable. The silence between us grew heavier, each vow binding us not out of love but out of duty, a contract we were both powerless to refuse. The gravity of her words, the emptiness in her voice, cut through me, and I felt a pang of guilt deep in my chest.

When it came time to lift her veil, I hesitated. I raised the delicate lace with unsteady hands, revealing her face, her expression etched in stone. Her eyes met mine, dark and guarded, her lips pressed into a firm line. Her gaze lingered, scanning my face as if searching for something—perhaps reassurance, perhaps a hint of doubt. But whatever it was, I felt I'd already failed her. There was nothing I could say that would make this right. The distance between us felt vast, insurmountable, a chasm that neither of us knew how to bridge.

The vicar cleared his throat, pulling us back into the moment, and I took her hand in mine, my thumb brushing over her glove in what I hoped might be a comforting gesture. But she pulled her hand back ever so slightly, her shoulders drawing up, as if any display of tenderness would only deepen her resentment. I could feel the wall between us growing higher, and the hopelessness of it all settled deep in my bones.

The kiss came next, and it was no more than a brief touch of lips, formal, devoid of sentiment. I felt her stiffen, her posture a silent resistance to the closeness forced upon us, and the message was clear: she would fulfill this role, but she would not surrender an inch of herself in doing so. It was a kiss that marked a boundary rather than a union, a reminder of the cold reality we were both trapped in.

The applause came, a muted murmur that echoed through the chapel, and I couldn't shake the feeling that we were performers on a stage, delivering a scene that had been scripted long before either of us had arrived. The guests rose, some smiling politely, others casting pitying glances our way, as if they, too, understood the hollowness of the spectacle. I wished, in that moment, that I could disappear, that the weight of their expectations could simply vanish, leaving me free of the burden I had never wanted.

As we turned to make our way down the aisle, arm in arm, I felt her tension, her arm barely brushing mine. It was as if she were trying to disappear, to become invisible, a shadow moving beside me rather than a partner in this new life. I could feel her resentment, the silent anger simmering beneath her composed exterior, and the guilt in my chest twisted painfully. I knew she hated this arrangement. And perhaps, in some hidden corner of myself, I hated it too.

We emerged into the open air, the muted sun casting a cold light over the stone steps. She looked straight ahead, her gaze fixed on some point beyond the horizon, her expression distant, impenetrable. The cheers from the gathered crowd felt distant, like a sound from another world, one that had no bearing on the reality we faced.

I leaned closer, lowering my voice. "Jemima," I murmured, hoping to offer some semblance of comfort, though I hardly knew what to say. "I understand this isn't what you wanted. But I promise, I will do all in my power to make sure you are comfortable, to honor you as best I can."

She looked up at me, her gaze sharp and piercing, and for a moment, I saw the flash of suspicion there once more. "Comfort," she echoed, the word falling from her lips like a cold, hard stone. She looked away before I could respond, her posture as rigid as ever. "That is all we shall have, Your Grace."

Her tone stung, a reminder that we were bound by duty, nothing more. Her words hung in the air between us, a reminder of the emptiness this marriage had brought upon us both. We were bound not by choice but by obligation, and in that moment, I realized just how vast the chasm between us truly was.

As we descended the steps together, with our guests watching in somber silence, I felt as though I were leading her not into a life of joy, but into a lifetime of restraint, of quiet resentment that would haunt us both.

10

A Distant Union

The journey from the chapel back to Wellesley Manor was quiet, save for the rhythmic clop of hooves on the gravel road. Jemima sat across from me in the carriage, her face turned toward the window, her gaze fixed on the passing countryside as though it held some hidden answer to the fate we both now shared. I tried to think of something to say, but every word felt hollow before it even formed. She'd hardly looked at me during the ceremony, and now, as we traveled deeper into the heart of my estate, the silence between us seemed like a chasm I could never cross.

As we pulled into the long, tree-lined drive, the manor loomed in the distance—a grand, gray stone testament to the Wellesley legacy. I glanced at Jemima, wondering what she might think of her new home, but her expression remained closed, her gaze shielded from me by that familiar, steely composure. The carriage slowed as we reached the entrance, and I could already see the line of servants gathered in anticipation, awaiting their new duchess.

I stepped out first, then offered her my hand as she alighted. She took it briefly, her fingers cold, her touch barely a whisper before she released it. She stood beside me, every inch a Duchess, her posture impeccable, her expression serene but distant as she faced the awaiting staff. One by one, I introduced her to the head servants—the butler, Mr. Howson; the housekeeper, Mrs. Leland; and the footmen and maids who would see to the day-to-day running of the household.

When we reached the final member of the line, a young maid with a soft face and gentle manner, I gestured toward her. "This is Mary," I said, inclining my head in Jemima's direction. "She will serve as your personal maid and assist you in any way you need."

Mary stepped forward and curtsied, her eyes lowered with respectful deference. "It is an honor, Your Grace," she said softly.

Jemima nodded in acknowledgment, her response courteous yet impersonal. I wondered if the same chill I felt coursed through her as well, the weight of our union settling like an invisible chain binding us both. After the introductions were complete, Jemima was shown to her quarters, where she would settle in and prepare for the evening.

The hours passed in a blur, filled with the quiet bustle of servants and the faint hum of the household returning to order. And then, as the evening descended, the realization settled over me: tonight was our wedding night.

The very thought made my pulse quicken with unease. There was no joy, no anticipation—only a gnawing sense of obligation and dread, a reluctance that went bone-deep. I could only imagine what she felt, what thoughts might have crossed her mind as she'd readied herself, alone in that vast, silent room. I felt a swirl of emotions—duty, guilt, even a flicker of fear. This was supposed to be a moment of unity, a beginning, yet all I felt was a sense of impending failure.

A knock at the door drew my attention. It was Mary, looking nervous as she informed me that the Duchess's room was prepared for the night. I nodded, dismissing her with a brief "Thank you," and felt the weight of the moment descend fully, pressing in from all sides.

I made my way to Jemima's room, my footsteps echoing down the quiet corridor. I knew what was expected of me, what tradition and society demanded. This was the night we were to consummate our marriage, to solidify the bond that had been spoken in vows. And yet, the closer I came to her door, the more the thought of it felt wrong—artificial. A ceremony atop a ceremony, forced and hollow. I felt a knot of uncertainty tightening in my chest, a sense of inadequacy that I couldn't shake.

I knocked, waited, and then entered.

Jemima stood by the window, her back to me, her shoulders tense beneath the soft folds of her gown. She turned at the sound of the door, her gaze meeting mine for a brief, charged moment. I saw the guarded look in her eyes, a flash of something that could have been fear or defiance, but was most certainly not warmth. Her eyes were dark, unreadable, and I couldn't help but feel that I was an intruder, an unwelcome presence in her space.

The silence stretched, heavy and thick, and I forced myself to speak. "Jemima," I began, choosing my words carefully, "it is tradition... that tonight we..." I trailed off, the words sounding foolish even to my own ears. I hated the way they felt, as if I were reading from a script, detached and insincere.

Her eyes narrowed slightly, a flicker of something cold passing over her face. "Must we?" she asked quietly, her voice calm, controlled.

I searched her face, seeing the tightly reined emotions, the reluctance mirrored in her expression. Her question hung between us, and in that moment, I knew that this night would be nothing more than another empty ritual, a duty neither of us truly wished to fulfill.

"No," I said finally, the word escaping in a soft breath. "No, we don't."

Her expression relaxed ever so slightly, but there was no gratitude in her gaze, only a kind of weary relief. I felt an odd pang at the sight, a strange mixture of disappointment and release. I didn't want to be the cause of her discomfort, and yet, I couldn't deny that her rejection stung, if only because it confirmed how vast the gulf between us truly was. I wanted to reach out, to bridge the distance somehow, but I knew that anything I did would only feel forced, unwanted.

"To avoid questions..." I continued, my voice low, "we'll say that... well, that you're indisposed. No one will think twice about it."

She gave a small nod, understanding, though her gaze remained averted. "Thank you," she murmured, the words barely more than a whisper. I knew then that she would never look at me with warmth, that our marriage was to be one of convenience and necessity, nothing more. The realization settled heavily in my chest, a hollow ache that I couldn't ignore.

"Good night, Jemima," I said quietly, taking a step back.

I left her standing there, a solitary figure framed by the dim light of the window, her gaze distant. As I closed the door behind me, I felt a weight lift from my shoulders, but it was swiftly replaced by a sense of hollowness, a reminder of the distance that separated us, a distance that was as much my doing as hers. I had wanted to be the man she could lean on, the man who could offer her comfort, but it seemed that I was already failing.

Back in my study, I sank into the leather chair by the hearth, turning my attention to the pile of correspondence and ledgers awaiting my review. The work was familiar, straightforward, a welcome reprieve from the confusion and unease that my new role as husband brought. As I delved into the figures and records, I tried to quiet my mind, to distract myself from the ache of a marriage that felt as lifeless as the empty halls of Wellesley Manor.

For hours, I worked by the dim light of a single lamp, the silence of the house pressing in from all sides. But no amount of ledgers or correspondence could dispel the nagging thought that I had somehow already failed—failed to offer her the comfort I'd promised, failed to bridge the gap between us. I felt torn between the sense of duty that had driven me to this point and the growing realization that I might never be the husband she needed, that I might never be able to fill the void left by Simon.

Outside, the night deepened, and the silence grew, echoing through the empty rooms, reminding me that for all my titles, for all my duty, I was as alone as I had ever been.

11

The Ties That Chafe

Wellesley Manor was colder than I had imagined. I'd known it would be grand and intimidating—imposing, even. It was a structure meant to showcase the wealth and status of the Wellesley family, a place that declared its owner's power from every corner and hall. But I hadn't anticipated the silence, nor the way it seemed to weigh on every room, filling the vast, empty spaces with an almost tangible chill. The walls seemed to absorb sound rather than reflect it, casting back only the faintest echoes of footsteps or the quiet shuffle of servants moving through the corridors.

The first days passed in a blur of introductions and half-hearted attempts to settle in. Josiah assigned me a maid, a young woman named Mary, who seemed more accustomed to silence than conversation. Her quiet presence was like the house itself—obedient, restrained, and entirely impersonal. She was diligent in her duties, anticipating my needs without a single misplaced word, but I quickly realized that Mary, like everyone else here, was not to be confided in.

After our arrival, I'd expected at least an effort at communication, an attempt to make this union into something more than formality. But the night of our wedding had made his intentions—or lack thereof—abundantly clear. He hadn't forced anything, hadn't made any demands, and though I should have been grateful for his restraint, it only left me feeling... dismissed.

As if my presence, my very existence, meant so little to him that he hadn't bothered to even acknowledge it.

As for Josiah... he was as distant as the manor walls.

He rose early, the faint sound of his movements drifting down the hall long before dawn, and by the time I emerged for breakfast, he was already gone. His schedule was precise, almost military in its discipline; I could have set the clocks in the manor by his daily routine. From breakfast to his afternoon hours in the study, from his quiet dinners to the late nights spent working by the light of a single lamp, his life was carved out in orderly, separate pieces. And, as I quickly came to understand, none of those pieces included me.

I caught glimpses of him throughout the day, his expression a mask of calm concentration, his attention forever occupied by letters, ledgers, and affairs of the estate. Each time we exchanged a few brief words, I felt the same impersonal courtesy, the same careful distance. It was as if he were merely performing his duty as a husband by occasionally checking in with me, a polite yet distant acknowledgment of my presence without any true interest. I began to wonder if he felt anything at all or if he was merely going through the motions, like a man dutifully tending to a task he neither enjoyed nor despised.

Wellesley Manor, too, seemed to mirror his disposition. The rooms were vast, grandly decorated, yet devoid of any warmth or personality. They were filled with furniture that looked as though it had been selected more for appearances than for comfort, as if the house itself were dressed in finery for the sole purpose of impressing guests who rarely, if ever, visited. I wandered through the halls, trailing my fingers over the smooth surfaces, each piece polished to an impersonal sheen. Nothing in the manor suggested that it was a home; rather, it felt like a monument to an unfeeling legacy, a relic preserved without thought for the lives that were meant to inhabit it.

The days stretched on, one after another, the silence growing heavier with each passing hour. I found myself listening to the faintest sounds—the creak of floorboards, the distant ticking of a clock, the soft rustle of Mary's skirts as she moved about her duties. Even the servants seemed to speak in hushed tones, as if they, too, were afraid of disturbing the oppressive quiet that had settled over the manor. Each night, as I lay alone in the vast bed, the darkness around me felt like a tangible presence, pressing down, suffocating.

I tried to distract myself, to find some sense of purpose or comfort, but every attempt felt as hollow as the walls that surrounded me. I'd thought I might find solace in the library, with its towering shelves and endless rows of books, but even there, the silence seemed to seep in, rendering the pages lifeless. I would select a book, flip through the pages, and find that the words slipped through my mind like sand, leaving nothing but an ache of loneliness that refused to fade.

Sometimes, in the solitude of my room or during the long, silent dinners, I found myself wondering how different things might have been if I had married Simon instead. I imagined a life filled with warmth and laughter, the kind of love that grew with each passing day rather than withered in silence. Simon would have made Wellesley Manor a home, not just a grand, empty shell. I pictured him teasing me over breakfast, leaning across the table to steal a bite from my plate, his eyes alight with mischief. He would have whispered in my ear as we walked through the gardens, his arm draped casually around my shoulders, his warmth chasing away the chill that now seemed to settle in my bones.

Simon would have filled these halls with joy. The servants would have smiled as they went about their duties, their laughter echoing softly through the corridors. We would have hosted gatherings, dinners filled with conversation and music, the house alive with the sounds of people, of life. And in the evenings, he would have held me close, his presence a constant reassurance, a reminder that I was not alone. I imagined his hand warm in mine, his voice soft as he spoke of our plans for the future, his love something tangible that I could hold onto.

But instead of Simon, there was Josiah—silent, distant, as cold as the stone walls of Wellesley Manor. He made no attempt to bridge the gap between us, no effort to turn this arrangement into something more than a contract fulfilled. The life I had imagined with Simon felt like a cruel mirage, something bright and beautiful that had been within reach, only to dissolve, leaving behind the emptiness of what now existed.

One afternoon, as I moved through the east wing, I heard the faint, rhythmic tapping of Josiah's pen against his desk. I paused, glancing through the slightly open door of his study, catching sight of him as he sat at his desk, his face drawn in concentration. The light from the window cast him in a sharp, angular profile, and for a brief moment, I felt a strange pang—a longing to know what went on behind that carefully controlled expression, to know if he ever felt even a fraction of what I felt.

But the thought faded as quickly as it came. His distance was as much a part of him as his title, and I could see now that he wore his role like armor, shielding himself from anything that might break through that reserved exterior.

Our interactions grew shorter, more formal, each one a reminder of the chasm between us. I became convinced that he saw me as an inconvenience, a necessary fixture he had inherited, just as he had inherited the title and estate. Perhaps he viewed our marriage as nothing more than an extension of his duties, an obligation he would fulfill out of respect for his brother's memory, but nothing more. He made no attempt to connect, no gesture of companionship or even shared understanding.

And so, I came to accept that this was my life now—a life bound by duty, devoid of warmth, where each day felt more like a sentence handed down rather than a choice freely made.

One evening, as we sat across from each other at the dinner table, the silence stretched unbearably. I glanced at Josiah, watching him as he carefully cut his food, his expression as closed off as ever. He didn't look up, didn't offer even a hint of conversation, and a feeling of entrapment tightened around my chest, cold and suffocating.

Finally, I couldn't bear it any longer. "Your Grace," I said, my voice louder than I'd intended, breaking the silence with an almost desperate edge. "Is there... anything you wish for me to do here? Any responsibilities you'd like me to take on?"

He looked up, his expression briefly surprised, as if he hadn't expected me to speak. For a moment, something flickered in his eyes—a flash of emotion, perhaps—but it vanished as quickly as it had come.

"Duties?" he repeated, his tone polite yet distant. "You are the Duchess, Jemima. You may do as you see fit."

The words were a dismissal, plain and simple. I felt my throat tighten, the rejection settling deep within me, mingling with the resentment that had been quietly growing since the day of our wedding. He had no interest in building a life with me, no desire to create a partnership, however formal. To him, I was a figurehead, a title, an obligation he would tolerate but never embrace.

The realization stung, a sharp reminder of the life I'd once envisioned and how far it had drifted from reality. With Simon, I had imagined laughter, companionship, a marriage that held both warmth and respect. But with Josiah, there was only this—an endless succession of days spent in silence, each one more isolating than the last.

As I looked down at my plate, my heart heavy, I realized that I was trapped in a gilded cage, bound to a man who saw me as little more than a necessity. The ties that bound us felt like chains, and with each passing day, I felt myself slipping further and further away from the woman I had once been.

The silence resumed, colder and more suffocating than before, and I forced myself to finish the meal, each bite tasteless, each moment another reminder of the emptiness that had taken root in my life.

12

Unfamiliar Territory

Wellesley Manor had never felt as vast and desolate as it did now. My days as Duke were filled with tasks and decisions—hours spent reviewing ledgers, managing tenants, meeting with stewards. These duties were expected, certainly, but what I hadn't expected was how easily they took on Simon's old shape, how each responsibility seemed to remind everyone, including me, of the brother I was trying to replace. I'd grown up in Simon's shadow, but now that shadow loomed darker and longer, its presence sharper in every interaction, every reminder of what the estate had lost.

And as husband to Jemima, I felt more uncertain than ever.

Her distance was palpable, a barrier of ice that neither of us dared to cross. I could see the resentment in her eyes whenever our paths crossed, the way she tensed if I so much as entered the same room. I'd tried, cautiously, to offer her small comforts—a new maid at her disposal, adjustments in her quarters, the luxury of privacy. But every time I made even a tentative gesture, her expression would tighten, as if any effort on my part to reach her was a nuisance she had no intention of acknowledging.

Respect, I told myself. Respect was all I could offer. She had no obligation to accept me, and I had no intention of forcing my presence upon her. But that didn't stop the tension that lingered between us, a constant, unspoken reminder of all we had been forced into.

In the few moments we spent together, over brief, silent dinners or accidental encounters in the halls, I felt her eyes on me, watchful and wary. Her gaze was as sharp as it was cold, a study in disdain she never bothered to conceal. I felt the sting of that disdain more than I wanted to admit, and the realization stung further still. How was it that this life, this title, this union—all meant to honor Simon—left me feeling so stripped of honor myself?

I'd chosen silence, hoping that if I gave her enough space, if I remained steady and respectful, she might come to understand that I was here not out of choice but of duty. But it was growing difficult to ignore the rumors, the unspoken words that seemed to circle us like vultures waiting to descend. They drifted through the servants, through the whispers of townsfolk when I ventured into town, the edges of conversations that halted whenever I drew near.

One morning, as I crossed the estate grounds on my way back from the village, I overheard two tenants speaking in hushed tones near the stables. They were discussing, without realizing I was within earshot, the tales that had resurfaced following my marriage to Jemima.

"I hear the new Duke still keeps company with the ladies," one of them murmured, her voice a mix of scandal and satisfaction, as if she enjoyed the taste of the gossip on her tongue. "And there's that talk of the child—bastard or not, it's no surprise the new Duchess seems unhappy."

The other tenant, an older man, gave a small grunt. "A shame," he replied. "One would think the Duke would take better care of his own family than keep to those old habits."

I paused, every muscle tensing, the air thickening around me as the words sank in. This was what they thought of me—that I was a man who cared only for his reputation, for the title, while keeping my wife in the dark with secrets of my own? They couldn't have been further from the truth, yet I felt no urge to defend myself, no words that could undo the damage done by years of assumption.

Simon. It had all been Simon. The reckless behavior, the rumors of women and a child left hidden from society—all shadows that my older brother had cast in his wake. But he'd left no room for clarity, no way to untangle the truth from the lies, and I was left bearing his legacy, a legacy Jemima seemed all too eager to believe.

I forced myself to continue on, my steps measured, my expression impassive. There would be no use confronting the tenants, no satisfaction in correcting their whispers. Any attempt to explain would likely sound defensive, desperate even, and would serve only to deepen the rumors. I'd already grown accustomed to the silent judgments, the knowing glances cast my way in the rare moments I appeared in town. And now, it seemed, Jemima herself must have heard the rumors as well.

In the study that afternoon, I found myself staring out the window, my mind caught in a loop of thoughts I couldn't quiet. Did she truly believe the worst of me? I'd hoped she might see through the fabrications, might see me for the man I was, not the man Simon had been. But her icy demeanor, her aversion, her silence all confirmed what I feared—she saw me as nothing more than the sum of those whispers.

I had spent my life trying to live with integrity, to honor my family name in a way that Simon had never cared to. And yet, for all my efforts, I felt as though I were constantly shadowed by his sins, trapped in a legacy that tainted everything I tried to build. With Jemima, I had hoped for a small reprieve, a chance to redefine what we could be. But the more I tried, the further she withdrew, and I felt the weight of every rumor, every unspoken judgment like stones gathering in my chest.

My thoughts drifted back to her, the cool indifference in her eyes whenever she looked my way. What did she see when she looked at me? A stranger in her husband's clothing, the ghost of the man she had expected to marry? I found myself thinking of ways I might explain myself, words I might use to defend my own honor, to tell her that everything she'd heard was nothing but a lie, a remnant of a brother who had left nothing but trouble in his wake.

But how would she even believe me? Would she see it as desperation, an attempt to excuse my own faults? The doubt gnawed at me, sharp and unrelenting, until I was left with only one thought: Jemima would have to see my character on her own terms. I would have to earn her respect, her understanding, not through explanation, but through patience.

The next question was, if I explained everything to her so that she could get to know the real me, would it mean anything to her?

I laughed softly, because I already knew the answer. Whether I was good or bad, real or apparent, nothing would change, because to her I would never be anything but a replacement husband.

With a sigh, I leaned back in my chair, staring at the endless rows of ledgers stacked around me. I'd always thought the duties of a Duke would be labor enough. I hadn't counted on the loneliness, on the battle to maintain my dignity amidst rumors and ghosts of a man I could never be. I'd hoped, foolishly perhaps, that Jemima might see me—truly see me. But it seemed she, like everyone else, was content to judge me through the eyes of a past I'd never wanted to inherit.

I returned to the ledgers, letting the familiar rhythm of numbers and calculations steady me. If my actions were all I could control, then I would let them speak for me. I would remain dignified, steady, and unfaltering, regardless of the judgments cast in my direction. It was a quiet resolve, but it was all I had left. And perhaps, one day, that resolve might be enough to show Jemima that I was not the man she believed me to be.

13

Misinterpreted Silence

The silence between us was slowly taking on a life of its own.

It was in the way Jemima's gaze flicked away whenever I entered a room, in the tension that filled the space between us like a thick fog. She moved through the manor with careful precision, her presence delicate but guarded, as if she feared a single misplaced word might shatter the uneasy peace we'd established. I'd hoped time would soften her demeanor, that she might come to see me as more than an obligation. But the silence between us only seemed to deepen with every passing day.

I often saw her seated in the drawing room, her posture rigid, her eyes fixed on some point beyond the window. Once, I had gathered the courage to approach, intending to ask if she might join me for a walk through the gardens, hoping for even the faintest sign of warmth. But as I neared, she'd turned away, her expression unreadable, her hands clenched in her lap. It was clear she had no interest in my company, and I had no desire to intrude where I wasn't wanted.

The rumors had begun to reach me, seeping through the manor walls like an unwelcome draft. The servants, careful as they were, could not fully hide the whispers that trailed behind them—the tales of my supposed indiscretions, of an illegitimate child that haunted the estate like a ghost from my past. They were the remnants of Simon's misdeeds, yes, but with him gone, I had become the natural subject of speculation, the convenient scapegoat.

Once, as I passed the kitchens, I heard the hushed voice of one of the maids. "It's no wonder the Duchess keeps her distance," she murmured to another servant. "With a husband like that, who can say where his loyalties lie?"

I paused just outside the door, my hands tightening at my sides. The other servant muttered a vague agreement, but I had heard enough. My blood simmered with a frustration I could not voice. I've been patient, but I can't hold it in anymore. How could I explain? To set the record straight would sound defensive, even desperate, and would only add fuel to the flames. And Jemima—God, did she believe these tales as well?

The thought haunted me, gnawing at the edges of my resolve. But every time I considered breaking the silence between us, every time I thought to address the rumors with her, I was held back by the fear that any attempt would make things worse. I'd hoped she might see through the falsehoods on her own, but with each day that passed, I could feel her growing more distant, her doubts fed by my silence. I didn't know how to tell her that I feared her rejection more than I feared the rumors.

During this time, I did nothing. I said nothing. And the silence between us grew. But I can't take this any longer, so I decided to try and speak with her over dinner, to bridge the silence that had grown between us. As we sat across from each other at the long dining table, the air between us felt as cold as the stone walls of Wellesley Manor. I watched her, trying to find the right words, the right way to begin. Jemima's eyes were focused on her plate, her expression closed off, her posture rigid.

"Jemima," I began, my voice hesitant, almost lost amidst the clinking of cutlery. She looked up briefly, her gaze meeting mine for just a moment before flickering away. "Is there... is there anything I can do to make you more comfortable here?"

Her eyes flicked back to me, cool and distant, as if she were assessing whether my question was genuine or simply another hollow attempt at civility. "No, Your Grace," she replied, her tone polite but devoid of warmth. "Everything is quite satisfactory."

The formality of her words stung, a reminder of just how far apart we were. I wanted to press further, to ask if she had heard the rumors, if she believed them, but the coldness in her demeanor stopped me. She seemed so uninterested, so detached, that I couldn't help but think she didn't care at all. Perhaps to her, I was just a stand-in for the man she had truly wanted—a man who was now gone.

I swallowed, nodding, trying to mask the disappointment that settled like a weight in my chest. "Very well," I said quietly, turning my attention back to my meal. The silence that followed was heavier than before, thick with all the words left unspoken.

I wondered if she even cared about the rumors, or if they simply confirmed what she already thought of me—that I was nothing more than a shadow of Simon, a duty she had to endure. The thought made my chest tighten, a mix of frustration and helplessness that I couldn't shake. I had tried to respect her space, to give her time, but it seemed that no matter what I did, I would never be more than an obligation to her.

The rest of the dinner passed in strained quiet, each moment dragging on with an unbearable slowness. I wanted to reach her, to find some way to break through the walls she had built, but I didn't know how. And her cold demeanor, her refusal to let me in, made me question if there was even a chance for us at all.

When the meal was finally over, Jemima rose from her seat, offering me a curt nod before excusing herself. I watched her leave, the door closing softly behind her, and I was left alone in the vast, empty dining room. The loneliness settled over me like a shroud, the silence echoing in the hollow space she'd left behind.

I leaned back in my chair, exhaling slowly, my gaze drifting to the flickering candlelight. I had wanted to talk to her, to bridge the gap between us, but it seemed that every attempt only pushed her further away. Perhaps, to her, I really was nothing more than a replacement—a reminder of what she had lost, and what she would never have again.

The silence between us was no longer just an absence of words; it had become a presence of its own, a barrier that neither of us seemed able to break. And as I sat there, alone in the dim light of the dining room, I couldn't help but wonder if this was how it would always be—two strangers bound by duty, forever separated by the ghost of a man neither of us could forget.

* * *

One evening, unable to bear the weight of my own thoughts, I rode out to the neighboring estate where my oldest friend, Benjamin, lived. Ben had been my friend for years, one of the few who had known both Simon and me, and understood the twisted web I was caught in. As I approached the warm glow of his manor, a sense of relief washed over me, as if I might finally find some reprieve from the endless restraint that bound me.

Ben greeted me at the door, his familiar smile offering a brief but welcome comfort. He led me to the library, where he poured two glasses of whiskey. The room was cozy, filled with the scent of old leather and warm wood, the fire casting flickering shadows on the shelves. Ben handed me a glass and settled into his armchair, regarding me with quiet patience, waiting for me to speak.

"You look like a man bearing the weight of the world," he said after a long silence, leaning back, his gaze fixed on me. "What's troubling you, Josiah?"

I took a slow sip of the whiskey, letting its warmth settle in my chest before replying. "It's Jemima," I admitted, my voice barely above a murmur. "I've tried, Ben. I've tried to be respectful, to give her space. But it feels like every step I take just pushes her further away."

Ben studied me, his gaze thoughtful. "She lost Simon," he said gently, nodding as if trying to piece it all together. "And now she's married to his brother, a man she barely knows. It must be difficult for her."

I let out a bitter laugh, the sound harsh in the quiet room. "Oh, I understand that. Believe me, I never wished to replace Simon. But she looks at me like I'm some kind of monster, like I... like I'm Simon himself, with all his faults and sins."

Ben frowned, his brow furrowing. "Are you talking about the rumors?"

I nodded, the word heavy as it escaped my lips. "Yes. The stories that have followed me since I took the title. They were Simon's doing—his indiscretions—but now, with him gone, the ton has latched onto me. I've become the easy target, the convenient scapegoat for everything he did." I hesitated, the frustration bubbling up. "And Jemima, she must have heard them too. I can't tell if she believes them or if she even cares enough to form an opinion."

Ben was silent for a moment, watching me with sympathy. His gaze held no judgment, just the kind of understanding only an old friend could offer. "You've always had a habit of taking on burdens that aren't yours, Josiah," he said finally, his tone gentle. "But maybe… maybe your silence is making things worse this time."

I looked at him, the confusion and frustration clear in my eyes. "You think I should confront her? Defend myself? I mean, I tried talking to her, Ben. Last night, I tried to ask if there was anything I could do, anything at all to make things easier for her. And you know what she did? She looked at me with that cold, indifferent stare, like she couldn't care less if I was even there. She said everything was fine, that there was nothing she needed, but I could tell she just wanted me to stop talking"

Ben took a sip of his whiskey, his eyes never leaving mine. "I think," he said slowly, "that Jemima is a woman who's found herself in a world she didn't choose, bound to a man she doesn't know. And I think she's as lost in all of this as you are. Maybe if she heard your side of things—truly heard it—she might see you for who you really are, not the man everyone assumes you to be."

I shook my head, doubt gnawing at me. "But what if it only makes things worse, Ben? What if she just thinks I'm trying to justify myself, or worse, making excuses for everything she's heard?" I sighed, the weight of it all pressing on my chest.

Ben smiled faintly, a touch of warmth and reassurance in his eyes. "Then at least she'll know you tried, Josiah. You're a man of integrity, but she won't see that if you keep hiding behind walls she can't break through. You need to let her see you, really see you. If she rejects that, then at least you'll know it wasn't for a lack of effort on your part. But right now, she needs to know who you are beyond the rumors, beyond the shadow of Simon."

The words struck me, the truth of them sinking deep. In my silence, in my endless restraint, I'd left Jemima alone to fend off the world's whispers, all while hoping she might somehow understand me without a word spoken. I had been a fool to think patience alone could bridge the chasm between us.

I drained the last of my whiskey, my thoughts turning over Ben's advice. There was no easy solution, no guarantee that a single conversation would undo the damage wrought by Simon's legacy. But for the first time, I felt a glimmer of resolve—a need to reach Jemima, to offer her something more than the silence that had defined us.

Ben clapped me on the shoulder as I rose to leave, his expression both reassuring and somber. "Whatever happens, Josiah," he said quietly, "she deserves to know the man she married."

Ben was right. Jemima deserved more than my silence, more than the rumors that haunted us both. Perhaps, in breaking that silence, I might find a way to reach her, to show her that there was more to me than the ghost of Simon's sins.

14

In the Shadows of What-If

Sometimes, when the house is still and the weight of silence fills every corner, I allow myself to wonder. What if I'd married Simon? What if he were still here, his laughter echoing down these halls, bright and warm? Would I be happier, tucked beneath his arm, sharing a life that promised warmth and adventure? Would he take me for walks every morning, lingering by the gardens to point out the wild roses that have become my favorite? Perhaps he'd kiss me by the rosebushes, unable to resist. Perhaps I'd distract him from his endless duties by perching on his lap, maybe even already be carrying his child, the morning sickness easier to endure because of his gentle reassurances.

The thought of Simon fills me with a mix of nostalgia and regret—a longing for something that never came to be, and a sorrow for the man who never had the chance to become my husband. I remember his carefree spirit, the way he could light up a room, the way his touch was always so sure, so comforting. It was a life I had imagined for myself, one filled with laughter, warmth, and affection. But those dreams were shattered the day Simon was taken from us, leaving behind a void that no one could fill—a void that I thought Josiah might, somehow, help me forget.

But my marriage to Josiah was nothing like that. There were no lingering walks, no stolen glances, and no warmth in the evenings. We exchanged only brief words at breakfast and dinner—careful pleasantries and polite inquiries that felt as rehearsed as the setting of the table. The rest of the day, Josiah was consumed by work. He poured over estate ledgers, read correspondence, met with tenants, and I—well, I was left to wander. There was no expectation, no duty for me beyond a simple, silent agreement that I'd married him and that was enough.

It was strange. In some ways, my life now felt like freedom—I could do as I wished, wander as I pleased, read, embroider, take tea, or walk for hours without anyone telling me otherwise. And yet, I felt caged. The boundaries were invisible, made not of chains but of indifference, held together by nothing more than a shared title. I'd thought we might slowly warm to one another, that time and proximity would melt the barriers between us. But Josiah seemed determined to keep his distance, an unspoken line drawn between his world and mine. He had erected walls so high that I couldn't see over them, and I'd grown too weary to try.

I'd heard the rumors, of course—of Josiah's supposed scandals, of a child he'd fathered out of wedlock. And yet, he hadn't so much as hinted at the truth of these tales, nor had he tried to explain them away. He remained silent on the matter, dignified, as though he didn't deem me worthy of knowing, as though whatever I thought simply didn't matter. It was a silence that spoke volumes—an unspoken confirmation that we were not partners, that we were, at best, cordial strangers.

This morning, a letter from my mother arrived, her words bursting with curiosity, the usual flurry of questions that pricked at old wounds. She asked about my health, about Josiah, about the household, but most pointedly, she asked about the possibility of grandchildren. She'd written, "How is your health, my dear? Surely there is news on the horizon, given you've been married for some time now. Tell me, is there already talk of a child?"

A child. My mother's eagerness jabbed at me, made sharper by the fact that the thought had not even crossed my mind since that first night. Since I'd refused Josiah in a fit of nerves and defiance, he hadn't pressed me. In fact, he'd moved quietly into the duke's quarters without so much as a word, as if that first refusal had settled things between us. Every night since, he'd retreated there, or perhaps to his study, and I'd only seen him in the mornings.

We lived separate lives beneath the same roof, and it seemed to suit him just fine.

I could picture my mother's face as she read my reply—one hastily written, filled with hopeful lies. I'd assured her that my marriage was fine and that news of a child would come soon enough. But as I penned the words, a strange chill ran through me. Was I fine? Was this... fine? Was this what marriage was supposed to be—two people living alongside one another, sharing a home but not a life?

After all, Josiah and I avoided each other as if we'd struck a mutual bargain to remain strangers. He buried himself in work, in duty, in anything that could fill his day, and I did the same with my solitude. Was this how he had envisioned marriage? Or had he, too, imagined something different, something more—something like the life I had once dreamed of with Simon?

I looked out the window, my hand resting on the sill, staring out at the manicured lawn that stretched toward the stables. Was I fooling myself, pretending we could stay like this forever—two people bound by obligation, avoiding each other in polite silence, waiting for something that might never come? I wanted more—I knew that now, with a clarity that frightened me. I wanted warmth, laughter, affection. I wanted the kind of love that made the mornings bright and the evenings bearable. I wanted a partner, not just in title, but in heart.

And yet, I didn't know if Josiah could ever be that for me. I didn't know if he even wanted to be. He was kind, yes, and patient, but there was a distance in his eyes, a guardedness that kept me at bay. I didn't know how to cross that distance, how to reach him, or if he even wanted me to. All I knew was that this—this half-life of politeness and distance—was not enough. Not for me. And maybe, just maybe, it wasn't enough for him either.

15

The Unwanted Gifts

It started with the books.

Mary brought them in one morning, a small stack tied neatly with ribbon, each volume carefully chosen. They were all of excellent quality, finely bound and clearly expensive—a new collection to add to the endless shelves of Wellesley's cold, formal library. At first, I thought perhaps Josiah had ordered them for himself, that he intended to retreat further into his studies. But Mary handed them to me, her voice quiet and polite, with a note attached, written in Josiah's unmistakable, tidy script.

To Jemima, in the hopes these volumes may brighten your days.

I turned the note over in my hands, feeling the smoothness of the paper, the clean ink that suggested care and thought. For a moment, I wondered why he had sent them. Was it an apology? A peace offering? Or perhaps, simply a duty? I remembered the conversation we had over dinner—one of the rare moments we attempted to speak beyond pleasantries. He had asked if there was anything he could do to make me more comfortable, and I had simply replied that I was fine.

The books themselves were harmless, a collection of poetry, natural history, and an illustrated guide to plants of England—a curious assortment that seemed to echo both the expected and the impersonal. As I leafed through them, I felt a flicker of something that could have been warmth, had I allowed it. Yet I quickly brushed it aside, telling myself it was merely a gesture. Polite, distant, and entirely devoid of emotion.

A few days later, another gift arrived.

This time, it was riding equipment: leather gloves, reins, a small toolkit for saddle care. The materials were fine, the leather supple, the craftsmanship impeccable. Clearly, Josiah had spared no expense. I couldn't deny the practicality of these gifts; the equipment was suited to long, quiet rides on the estate grounds. But there was something about the careful selection, the attention to detail, that felt hollow. It was as if he'd been advised on precisely what to give, as if he'd consulted some manual on how to be a dutiful husband rather than offering anything that spoke of genuine thought.

I ran my fingers over the smooth leather of the gloves, feeling a pang of frustration building within me. Gifts, no matter how costly or well-chosen, could not erase the emptiness of our shared life. They could not bridge the distance that seemed to grow wider with each passing day.

These gestures were precise, considered—almost cold. Did he truly believe that these items, these things, could substitute for actual words, for a genuine conversation? Did he think he could fulfill his role by simply filling my hands with trinkets?

"Is it not generous, Your Grace?" Mary asked as she quietly tidied the library, glancing at the latest addition—a lovely set of silk bookmarks he had included with the books. She had the look of one enchanted by the luxury of it all, her eyes bright with admiration. "The Duke must think highly of you, indeed."

I turned away from the stack, forcing a smile. "Yes, Mary, I suppose he does," I replied, but the words felt wrong, as hollow as the gifts themselves.

Why couldn't he offer something personal, something that might actually mean something to me? A note with more than mere pleasantries? A token from his own life, something that revealed even a hint of who he truly was beneath the polished surface? But no, Josiah seemed content to stay firmly behind his wall of formality, passing along expensive but impersonal tokens in place of actual sentiment.

I couldn't shake the feeling that this was all part of some elaborate performance, a routine of duty without any hint of warmth or sincerity. Was he simply maintaining appearances, fulfilling his role with cold precision? The thought churned uneasily within me, darkening my already troubled heart.

And yet... there was a flicker of something else, a question that nagged at the edges of my thoughts, unwelcome and uncertain.

The gifts were thoughtful. They were practical, yes, but tailored to my interests—the poetry, the guide to the estate plants, the riding gloves that fit my hands perfectly. There was an undeniable attention to detail, as though he had tried, in his own muted way, to offer me something he thought I might enjoy.

But then, why was he not here, sharing these things with me? Why leave the gesture without the connection? I felt torn, caught between frustration and a quiet, confusing ache. Perhaps I'd been too quick to assume his motives, to dismiss these gestures as mere formality. Perhaps he truly believed that these tokens, impersonal as they seemed, might bring me some small measure of happiness.

But no. That was foolish. He had plenty of chances to speak to me, to bridge the distance, and he'd chosen to keep his silence. I wasn't a fool. He was going through the motions, likely telling himself that these gestures would suffice, that he was fulfilling his duty well enough with gifts and notes and polite avoidance.

I tried to focus on other things, but the gifts gnawed at me, a reminder of the gap between us that seemed only to grow wider. They sat there, a silent accusation, each one hinting at the intimacy I craved and yet could never reach.

That evening, I caught a glimpse of him in the hallway. He was just leaving his study, his expression one of faint weariness, but he looked up as he saw me. For a moment, I wondered if he might stop, if he might say something—anything—that might break the barrier between us. But he merely inclined his head, offering a polite "Good evening, Jemima," before continuing on his way.

I felt the sting of it, sharper than I cared to admit. How could he be so perfectly polite, so carefully detached? How could he carry on with this formality, day after day, as if there were nothing between us but duty and expectation?

I wanted to call after him, to demand something—anything—that might feel real. But the words died in my throat, held back by a frustration I couldn't voice. How could I ask him for something I wasn't even sure he knew how to give?

I returned to my room, the latest gift still on my dresser, its pristine leather glinting faintly in the candlelight. I stared at it, feeling a swell of anger, an unbidden sadness creeping in as well. Did he truly think this was enough? Did he believe that these gestures, as polished and proper as they were, could replace the connection we both knew was missing?

I picked up the gloves, my fingers brushing over the leather, feeling the weight of my own frustration pressing down on me. Somewhere, in some part of myself that I tried to ignore, I felt a faint glimmer of understanding—a suspicion that perhaps, in his own awkward way, he was trying. That he didn't know how to bridge the chasm between us any more than I did, and so he offered what he could, however insufficient.

But that thought, fragile as it was, felt too dangerous to nurture, too vulnerable to hold onto.

So I set the gloves aside, turning away from the gifts, from the silent questions that filled my heart. I would not be distracted by vague hopes or half-imagined intentions. Until he proved otherwise, I would assume he was simply fulfilling his duty, nothing more.

And if that was all he could offer, then I would learn to live without expecting more.

16

The Glimpses of Integrity

The morning was unusually crisp, with the first hints of autumn whispering through the estate grounds, a reminder that even the seasons here were dictated by quiet, relentless order. I'd chosen to wander the grounds alone, feeling the weight of Wellesley Manor pressing down upon me like a physical presence. My frustrations with Josiah, his distance, and his infuriating politeness simmered beneath the surface, leaving me restless and unable to sit still in the silent, lifeless rooms.

As I wandered down a narrow path that led to the tenant cottages on the edge of the estate, I noticed a small group gathered by one of the homes. Josiah stood in the center, his back to me, tall and calm as he spoke with a family I didn't recognize—a mother and her two young children. The woman's face was creased with worry, her hands clutched tightly before her as if she were holding her whole world together by sheer will alone. She glanced up at Josiah, her expression hopeful and pleading, and I slowed my steps, curious despite myself.

"I'll see to it that you have enough to make it through winter," Josiah was saying, his tone gentle, yet resolute. "There's no need for you to worry. We'll arrange for additional provisions, and I'll ensure the necessary repairs are made to your roof before the rains set in."

The woman nodded, her shoulders sagging with visible relief. "Thank you, Your Grace," she murmured, a catch in her voice. "We... we've struggled so much this year, with my husband gone, and the harvest being what it was... I didn't know where else to turn."

Josiah reached out, placing a steadying hand on her shoulder, a gesture so natural, so kind, that it startled me. "You did the right thing in coming to me," he replied softly. "That's what I'm here for. We'll get through this, and next season will be better, I promise."

He spoke with a sincerity that seemed to cut through the chill of the morning, a warmth in his voice that I'd never heard in all our brief conversations. This wasn't the distant, polite Duke I knew from our cold, restrained marriage. This was a man of true conviction, someone who understood the burdens of others and who, in his quiet way, shouldered them without hesitation.

As I watched, the two children tugged at their mother's skirts, and she smiled down at them, her face softening. Josiah's gaze shifted, and he knelt to meet the children at their level. I found myself holding my breath, caught off guard by the gentle way he spoke to them.

"What are your names?" he asked, his voice lightening in a way I'd never heard before.

"Thomas," the older boy replied shyly, barely glancing up at Josiah. The younger, a girl no older than five, hid her face in her mother's skirts.

"Well, Thomas, I'll make sure you have some extra blankets for the cold months," Josiah said with a smile. "And perhaps we can find you some toys as well, hmm? To make the winter a little more cheerful?"

The boy's eyes widened, and his face broke into a tentative smile. His mother's eyes misted, gratitude evident as she glanced between her children and the Duke who had, for the moment, made their troubles his own. I felt something shift within me, an unexpected flicker of warmth for this man who had been nothing but a stranger in his own home. I'd spent so long resenting him, thinking him cold and indifferent, assuming that every gesture he made toward me was nothing but obligation.

But this... this was different. There was no one here to witness his kindness, no guests to impress, no social gain to be had from helping a tenant family on the fringes of the estate. This was something he did quietly, without expectation of recognition. And it was in that moment, as I watched him offer comfort and stability to those who depended on him, that I felt a glimmer of something I hadn't expected—respect.

As he rose to his feet, the family thanked him profusely, and he offered them a few final words of reassurance before turning back toward the manor. I instinctively moved to the side, hoping to avoid his gaze, but he caught sight of me. For a heartbeat, his expression shifted, surprise flashing in his eyes before he composed himself, his face slipping back into the careful neutrality I knew so well.

"Jemima," he greeted me, his tone polite as always, but there was a faint warmth lingering in his voice, a trace of the man I'd just seen with the tenants.

"I... I didn't mean to intrude," I replied quickly, suddenly feeling self-conscious. "I was simply out for a walk."

He nodded, his gaze flicking back toward the cottages. "They've had a difficult year," he said quietly, as if he owed me an explanation. "I do what I can to ease their burdens, but sometimes..." He trailed off, a shadow crossing his face, and for a moment, I saw a depth of emotion I hadn't thought him capable of.

"It seems you're doing more than enough," I managed to say, surprised at the words as they left my mouth. "They're lucky to have someone who cares so much for their well-being."

He glanced at me, a faint crease between his brows, as if my words had caught him off guard. "It's my duty," he said, but his tone lacked the usual formality, as if the phrase meant more to him than mere obligation.

We stood there in silence for a moment, an unexpected quiet falling between us that felt... different. Not strained, not filled with the resentment and judgment that had marked so many of our previous encounters. This silence felt more like understanding, as if we had both glimpsed something in the other that we hadn't seen before.

After a moment, he nodded again, his gaze holding mine for a fraction longer than usual. "If there's ever anything you need, Jemima," he said, his voice low, "please know that you can come to me."

It was a simple statement, nothing grand or overtly emotional. But for the first time, I felt the weight of those words, as if he were offering me something more substantial than the gifts he'd sent, more meaningful than the polite exchanges we shared over supper. He was offering me a choice—a chance to cross the distance between us, if I chose to take it.

"I'll... keep that in mind," I replied softly, unsure of how else to respond.

He inclined his head, then turned back toward the manor, his steps measured and steady as he walked away. I watched him go, feeling a strange mixture of emotions I couldn't quite name. Respect, certainly. But there was something else as well, a faint, growing warmth that had nothing to do with duty or obligation.

As I resumed my walk, my mind returned to the scene I had just witnessed, the genuine kindness he'd shown to the tenant family, the way he'd knelt to speak with the children, as if they were just as worthy of his attention as any member of the ton. I found myself wondering if perhaps I had misjudged him, if perhaps there was more to Josiah than I had allowed myself to see.

It was a troubling thought, unsettling in its implications. For so long, I had clung to my resentment, my assumptions about him, as a shield against the uncertainty of this marriage. But now, that certainty felt as fragile as glass, shattered by a single act of kindness.

I pushed the thought away, unwilling to confront the full depth of its meaning. But as I returned to the manor, I couldn't shake the image of him standing among his tenants, offering comfort with quiet integrity, a man who bore his responsibilities with a care I had never thought to attribute to him.

And though I tried to tell myself that this glimpse of him was nothing more than a fleeting moment, I knew, deep down, that something had changed. For the first time, I found myself wondering who my husband truly was—and whether, perhaps, he was a better man than I had ever believed possible.

17

An Unexpected Gesture

The rumors had resurfaced with a vengeance, as if the entire estate were holding its breath, waiting to see if the new Duke would live up to his predecessor's indiscretions. I'd spent years ignoring these whispers, knowing the truth well enough that their sting eventually dulled. But now, with Jemima by my side—distant, frosty, and so clearly disgusted by the very notion of our marriage—those rumors felt like thorns, sharper and harder to ignore.

They must have come from Simon, whispered into the wrong ears by a man who'd often done as he pleased, leaving me to inherit both his title and the sins he'd strewn carelessly in his wake. But how could I explain that to Jemima without it sounding like a cowardly excuse? How could I tell her that I'd spent a lifetime as Simon's scapegoat without appearing to drag my dead brother's name through the mud?

Instead, I resolved to let my actions speak for themselves, to prove through effort and sincerity that I was not the man she thought. And though I hadn't the faintest notion how to reach her, I decided to begin with a gesture—something that would demonstrate my regard for her in a way that mere words never could.

An idea took root. A small gathering, intimate but significant, where I might officially honor Jemima's place as the new Duchess of Wellesley. I wanted it to be warm and welcoming, a gentle introduction to her role, rather than the stiff, distant dinners we typically shared with strangers. And, if I were honest with myself, I wanted to create a memory with her—a moment unmarred by duty and formality.

I threw myself into the planning, working with the staff to make sure every detail was perfect. I chose delicate arrangements of her favorite flowers to decorate the dining room and personally reviewed the menu with the cook. I even instructed the musicians to prepare pieces that I thought Jemima might enjoy, something softer, perhaps even playful, to counter the somber air that hung over us both. As for the guest list, I kept it small and familiar, inviting only our closest family members.

When the evening arrived, the manor seemed almost transformed. Candlelight softened the grand hallways, casting a warm glow that softened the stone walls. I waited in the drawing room, anticipation building as I glanced at the doorway, hoping to see Jemima's reaction, to glimpse some spark of delight or even surprise in her expression.

She appeared soon enough, her figure framed in the doorway, her gown an elegant shade of blue that somehow made her look both regal and approachable. But as she stepped into the room, I could see the familiar guardedness in her gaze, a faint wariness that hinted at her unwillingness to engage, to risk any semblance of enjoyment.

The guests arrived shortly after, filling the room with laughter and polite conversation. I managed to catch Jemima's eye a few times, nodding subtly in what I hoped conveyed encouragement, though her responses were little more than brief glances and faint, polite smiles.

Just as I was beginning to think that my efforts might lead to some small change between us, the conversation turned, as it inevitably did, to the subject of an heir.

It was my aunt who broached the topic, her sharp gaze flicking between Jemima and me with a barely concealed impatience. "Well, it has been a respectable amount of time since the wedding, has it not?" she remarked, her voice carrying just enough volume to turn a few heads. "Surely there must be some news on the horizon."

A heavy silence fell, the unspoken expectations pressing down upon us both.

I glanced at Jemima, feeling a twinge of regret as I saw her jaw tighten, her hand clenching at her side. This was the last thing I had wanted for tonight, the last reminder of the duties and obligations that bound us together with such cold efficiency.

"We're in no rush, Aunt," I replied smoothly, keeping my tone light, though my patience was beginning to fray. "Jemima has only just settled into her role. There's ample time for all... expectations to be met."

The conversation shifted after that, but the damage was done. I could see Jemima retreating into herself, her eyes growing distant, her expression hardening as though she were drawing a veil around herself. I wanted to reach out, to say something that might ease her discomfort, but the words felt inadequate. My well-laid plans, my efforts to create an evening of warmth and acceptance, had crumbled in the face of a single comment.

After dinner, I found her alone in the library, her back to me as she gazed out the window. She hadn't heard me enter, and I hesitated, watching the way her shoulders rose and fell with each quiet breath, the tension radiating from her like an invisible shield.

"Jemima," I said softly, hoping not to startle her.

She turned, her expression neutral, though I could see the glint of frustration beneath her composed exterior. "Yes, Your Grace?" she replied, her tone carefully formal, as though we were nothing more than strangers sharing an awkward courtesy.

I took a step closer, my hands at my sides. "I wanted to apologize. This evening... I'd hoped it might make things easier for you. I never intended for the conversation to turn toward... expectations."

She watched me, her gaze unfathomable. For a moment, I thought I saw a flicker of something—sadness, perhaps, or disappointment—but it vanished as quickly as it had come.

"Thank you for the effort, Your Grace," she replied, her voice cool. "But I've long since accepted that my presence here is largely symbolic. The estate and its legacy are what truly matter."

I felt the sting of her words, sharper than I'd expected. "You are more than a symbol, Jemima," I said, a hint of frustration slipping into my tone. "If you would only let me—"

"Let you what?" she interrupted, her gaze hardening. "Let you prove that you are not the man they all believe you to be? I'm certain you've done that well enough for yourself, but I'm afraid actions speak louder than words. And so far, your actions... they've been respectable, but hardly revealing."

Her words cut deeper than I wanted to admit. I felt my jaw clench, an unexpected ache settling in my chest. I wanted her to see the sincerity behind my actions, to understand that this evening had been for her, not out of duty or obligation, but out of a desire to know her, to bridge the distance that had kept us apart.

"I only wish to make this easier for us both," I replied, my voice softer. "I thought... I thought you might appreciate the gesture."

For a moment, she held my gaze, and I saw the faintest flicker of uncertainty in her eyes. But it passed, her walls rising once more, her expression unreadable.

"It was a kind thought," she said quietly, turning her gaze back to the window. "But kindness and gestures cannot change what we are."

I wanted to argue, to tell her that it didn't have to be this way, that we didn't have to spend our lives circling each other, locked in this cold, endless distance. But I knew that any attempt to convince her would only push her further away. She had built her walls for a reason, and I had no choice but to respect them.

The silence stretched between us, thick and impenetrable. I felt the weight of my own frustration, my own longing, pressing down upon me, but I knew there was nothing more I could say. I'd tried, and I'd failed. And though I wanted to reach her, to show her that she was more than just a symbol in my life, I could only hope that one day, my actions might prove what words could not.

As I left the library, a heavy ache settled in my chest, a quiet longing that I couldn't shake. I had come into this marriage out of duty, but somewhere along the way, it had become more. Somewhere along the way, I'd begun to want her—to truly want her. And I couldn't ignore the quiet, painful truth that this feeling was unreciprocated, hidden behind walls I feared would never come down.

For the first time, I allowed myself to acknowledge the depth of my own desire, my own growing attachment to her, despite the walls she had built between us. And though I knew I couldn't force her to feel the same, I resolved to keep trying, to keep showing her, through patience and quiet gestures, that she was not alone in this life, that she was more than just an obligation or a title.

Perhaps, one day, she would see it.

18

A Necessary Sacrifice

The evening had unraveled in ways I hadn't anticipated. I'd intended to create a small gesture of warmth for Jemima, to show her that our marriage need not remain a hollow transaction. Yet despite every effort, the evening had ended with her colder than ever, each polite response layered with the bitterness she barely hid.

I should have been accustomed to this by now, to the silence that stretched between us and the layers of mistrust she wore like armor. But as I stared at the empty room, the warmth of my plans extinguished, I couldn't help but feel a growing frustration, an ache that ran deeper than I'd allowed myself to acknowledge before. Somewhere in the midst of our silent exchanges, I had begun to want something more from her—more than dutiful glances, more than cold acceptance. I wanted her trust, her companionship... and maybe even her affection.

And yet, she remained as closed off as ever, viewing our union as nothing more than a transaction. I could hardly blame her—my words and actions thus far had done little to suggest otherwise. We were a marriage of titles and duties, joined by nothing but obligation, and with each passing day, it seemed as though we were sinking further into that rut.

The whispers I'd overheard from the guests haunted me, my aunt's pointed question lingering like an accusation: *Surely there must be some news on the horizon.* The absence of an heir only worsened Jemima's position in my family, leaving her vulnerable to further speculation and rumor. What I had thought was giving her space, a way to respect her choices, had only stoked the gossip and placed her in a precarious position.

I drew in a deep breath, steeling myself, before crossing the room toward the library where she'd retreated earlier. My steps felt heavy, each one carrying the weight of the decision I had been reluctant to face. But avoiding this matter would only hurt her further, leaving her in a position as uncertain as it was untenable.

When I reached the doorway, I paused, finding her seated by the fire, her gaze distant, her shoulders squared as if she were readying herself for another onslaught of reminders and expectations. Her figure seemed impossibly small against the grand backdrop of the room, her hands clasped tightly in her lap, the usual guardedness etched into her features.

"Jemima," I said softly, and she turned to me, her expression unreadable, though I caught a flicker of something as her gaze settled on mine—perhaps resignation.

She straightened, giving me her full attention. "Why have you come, Your Grace?" she asked, her voice guarded, but there was a hint of curiosity beneath the layers of her usual detachment. Maybe she was confused because I hadn't been gone long and then came back.

I hesitated, searching for the right way to begin. "I... I wanted to speak with you about something important," I said, my voice careful.

Jemima tilted her head slightly, her expression still guarded. "What is it? What matter is so important that you came to find me?"

I hesitated, my fingers brushing against the back of a chair as if searching for the right words. I looked at her, unsure how to proceed, my brow furrowed slightly. I shifted my weight, glancing at the floor before meeting her gaze again. "I..." I started, then paused, rubbing the back of my neck, visibly struggling to find the right opening. After a moment, I finally spoke.

"It's about dinner conversation. I realize that we've delayed the matter of an heir," I continued, pausing to gauge her reaction, measuring each word. I paused, trying to gauge her reaction, measuring each word. "I thought I was respecting your choice by not pressing the issue. But after tonight, it's clear that this delay is causing more harm than good."

Jemima's expression remained still, her eyes on mine, but her guardedness softened just a fraction. I forced myself to continue, determined not to let this conversation become another cold exchange. "The Wellesley name requires an heir, and without one, I'm afraid your position... it's left vulnerable to speculation and criticism." I paused, searching her face for any sign of resistance, any indication that she would refuse.

But instead, she let out a soft sigh, her gaze falling to her hands. "You're right, Your Grace," she replied quietly. "I think I've known this was inevitable... but I kept pushing it away, perhaps out of fear." She met my gaze, her expression calm but resolute. "I apologize for delaying this for so long. And I... I thank you for your patience."

Her words took me by surprise, and for a moment, I could only stare at her, caught off guard by her acceptance. I had been expecting her to argue, to resist the very idea, and yet here she was, speaking with an understanding that left me feeling strangely unsettled.

"Jemima," I said slowly, the words hesitant, "this isn't... this isn't something I take lightly. I know what I'm asking of you." I swallowed, feeling an ache rise within me as I considered what this must mean for her—a woman who had lost one brother and was now bound to another, carrying a title that had come at such a cost. "I apologize too... for putting you through this, for placing this burden upon you. And for... for asking you to bring a child into the world in such a way."

She looked at me, her expression softening ever so slightly, though her gaze held a flicker of something I couldn't quite place. For a moment, I thought I saw an understanding there, a quiet acknowledgment of the choices neither of us had truly been given. "Thank you for saying that," she murmured, her voice quiet, steady. "But I understand that this is part of our arrangement."

Her words struck me, a quiet, unwelcome reminder of what our marriage had become—a transaction, a binding contract with terms neither of us could escape. I wanted to say something to dispel the coldness of it all, to tell her that it wasn't just about duty, that I was beginning to want something more. But as I looked at her, her face closed off once more, I realized that any such words would sound hollow, insincere. Perhaps that was what she saw me as—a man of duty and obligation, willing to ask her for the bare minimum but nothing more.

"Very well," I said finally, the words feeling heavier than I'd intended. "I will do my best to make this as… as manageable as possible for you." I hesitated, searching her face, wondering if there was anything else I could say that would somehow make this easier.

She gave me a faint, polite nod, her expression composed but unreadable. "I suppose that is all I can ask for, Your Grace."

The title felt like a knife, sharp and precise, cutting through any illusion that this was anything more than a duty we both shared. I turned, letting the silence settle between us, feeling an emptiness that seemed to stretch into every corner of the room.

And yet, even as I walked away, I felt the weight of her words linger, a quiet reminder that, for all the plans and titles that bound us, I was no closer to her heart than the day we'd wed. We were still strangers, tied together by obligations neither of us had wanted, trapped in a cage of expectation with no way out.

But I resolved, with a quiet desperation I dared not name, that I would continue to try. For as long as she remained by my side, I would show her, in whatever ways I could, that she was more than a title, more than an obligation. And perhaps, if I could not make her love me, I could at least give her a life that would not feel like a prison.

19

The Silent Bargain

The silence of the room seemed to echo with the unspoken, with everything we had agreed to without truly speaking the words. Josiah had gone, and yet his apology lingered in the air, clinging to me in a way I couldn't quite shake. He had apologized—apologized for needing to ask this of me, for making me bear the burden of bringing a child into this world. He had asked me for this duty, as though it were some painful task he regretted, and yet, wasn't it what I had been groomed for all my life? What I'd expected since the day I'd known I was to be a duchess?

Why, then, did his words feel like a wound, as if he had pressed against something raw within me? He'd apologized as though this act—this fulfillment of duty—was a weight he regretted placing upon me. And it struck me, deeply, that he hadn't even hinted at desire, hadn't given a word of warmth or comfort to ease the coldness of his request. I was merely to perform my role, to produce the heir that would secure his lineage, as if that was the sole purpose of my existence by his side.

The question lingered at the edge of my thoughts, persistent and unwelcome: *Did Josiah see me only as a tool? An instrument to fulfill his family's need for an heir?*

And then, perhaps cruelly, my mind dredged up the rumors, the whispers that had once been easy to ignore. *An illegitimate child,* they'd said. Some hushed tale of indiscretion and wild, hidden passions. Did he see me as nothing more than the mother of his next child? Did he assume I would perform this role without question, without need for explanation or care? A chill ran through me at the thought, at the sudden, horrible feeling that I was merely another transaction in his life.

My heart twisted in confusion and something that felt oddly like sadness—a sorrow that seemed misplaced, yet unshakable. Because as much as I might resent this situation, as bitter as the duty felt, there had been a tiny, fragile hope within me that perhaps, with time, Josiah and I could have forged something warmer, something shared. But his cold apology only confirmed what I had long feared: this marriage was, and would always be, little more than an obligation.

Yet, that didn't make sense, did it? He'd never spoken of this supposed child from his past, and I'd never dared to ask. If he truly had fathered an illegitimate child, then surely he understood the reality of parenthood already. But if that were true, why had he approached the idea of an heir with such distance, as though the very notion of it was something foreign to him?

I felt a pang of something like guilt mingling with confusion, a gnawing feeling I couldn't place. I'd built a wall between us, convinced that he was as cold and distant as I had first believed, but what if... what if there was more to it? What if, behind his mask of formality and reserve, there was a man as lost and uncertain as I was?

But what choice did I have? Simon's death had left us both ensnared in this strange, unyielding situation. I hadn't chosen Josiah, nor he me. We were only here because of a cruel twist of fate that had left him a title he hadn't wanted and me a life I hadn't asked for.

I drew in a shaky breath, the weight of it all settling over me like a shroud. My mother's voice echoed faintly in my memory, her stern insistence on duty, on fulfilling what was expected of me without question. *You're a duchess now,* she'd said. *You know what is required of you.*

And, logically, I did. There was nothing inherently wrong in Josiah's request. It was what was expected, what had always been expected. And yet, as I sat there, replaying his words, the unfeeling apology he'd given me, I couldn't shake the hollow ache that had settled within me.

A soft knock interrupted my thoughts, and I looked up to see Sarah, my maid, hovering in the doorway, her expression a mask of gentle concern.

"Is everything alright, my lady?" she asked softly, her eyes searching mine.

"Yes, Sarah," I replied, my voice sounding distant even to my own ears. "Everything is as it should be."

But as she retreated, I felt the falseness of my words, the lie heavy on my tongue. Because, in truth, nothing was as it should be. I was bound to a man who seemed as trapped as I was, both of us playing roles handed down to us without choice or question. And though I tried to steel myself, to remind myself that this was simply my duty, I couldn't deny the faint, unwelcome sadness that lingered within me.

If this was to be my life, I thought bitterly, then so be it. But as I glanced back at the empty room, my hands resting on my lap, I couldn't help but wonder what it would have been like if things had been different. If, perhaps, there had been warmth behind Josiah's request, a genuine care that might have softened the harshness of our reality. Maybe Josiah was trying to protect me like when Josiah calmed down the tenants and the little boy that day. Maybe there's another side of him that I don't know.

But as it was, all I could do was perform the duty expected of me, to fulfill my role with the same cold detachment that had become our unspoken agreement.

And maybe, just maybe, I could convince myself that it would be enough.

20

A Bitter Obligation

In the days following the gathering, an unsettling shift rippled through Wellesley Manor. Conversations halted as I passed, whispers trailing in my wake, quiet murmurs that I couldn't quite catch but understood all too well. The household was waiting, watching, as though we were a performance piece they'd paid to witness, with their expectations pressed upon me like a weight I could hardly bear.

I had no illusions about what they wanted. As the new Duchess, my purpose here was clear: to provide an heir, to ensure the continuation of the Wellesley line. It was a duty as old as the title itself, woven into the very fabric of my marriage. And as much as I had tried to ignore it, to evade the growing pressure with delayed evenings and flimsy excuses, the reality was becoming impossible to escape.

The household murmured about it openly now, discussing the consummation that had been so politely postponed. I heard the servants exchanging speculative glances, heard the head housekeeper muttering about the "duty of a Duchess." And though Josiah had never once pressed the matter—had, in fact, gone to great lengths to give me my own space and time—the choice no longer felt like mine to make. I was cornered by tradition, by duty, by the silent but relentless pressure from everyone around me.

And so, that evening, I found myself waiting, dressed in a nightgown that felt like little more than a symbol, a garment meant to signify my acceptance of this duty, of this life that felt increasingly like a cage.

When Josiah entered, he looked surprised to find me waiting, as if he hadn't expected that I'd finally relent. He paused, his gaze lingering on me, a flicker of uncertainty passing over his face before he schooled his expression into something unreadable.

"You don't have to..." he began, his voice quiet, almost hesitant. I could see the restraint in his posture, the way he kept his distance, as though he sensed my reluctance and wanted to offer me one last reprieve. "I mean we don't have to do it so soon."

But I couldn't delay any longer. "It's expected of us," I replied, my voice colder than I intended. I didn't look at him, didn't dare meet his gaze, for fear that he might see the resentment simmering just beneath the surface. "As you said before, delaying conjugal relations will only bring more threats."

He nodded slowly, the faintest trace of something—regret, perhaps—passing over his face. But he moved forward, and I steeled myself, bracing for what I knew would come.

As he reached for me, his touch was firm but careful, as if he were afraid of breaking something delicate. I felt the roughness of his hands, the heat of his skin, and my mind raced, instinctively recoiling from the intimacy that now felt unavoidable. I could feel the weight of my own resentment coiling within me, tightening like a vice as his hands slid over me, as he guided me to the bed with a tenderness that only seemed to deepen the ache of bitterness lodged in my chest.

I'd expected detachment, something quick and mechanical, but there was something else in his gaze, a fierceness that caught me off guard, that made my heart pound with a mixture of fear and something I couldn't name. His lips pressed against my skin, his breath warm and uneven, and I felt trapped beneath him, held captive by a man I barely knew, a man who had become both my husband and my captor in one unyielding role.

The intensity of it, the way he moved, felt wild, almost primal, and I found myself shrinking beneath him, wishing to disappear, to escape this arrangement that had become unbearably real. There was no romance here, no tenderness that might have softened the edges of my resentment. Instead, it felt harsh, a fulfillment of duty rather than any expression of affection. He was relentless, a force bearing down upon me, claiming a part of me I hadn't been ready to give, and I felt as if I were drowning beneath the weight of his presence, his power.

When it was over, he lay beside me in silence, his breathing still ragged, his hand resting lightly on my shoulder. I lay perfectly still, my body rigid and unyielding, staring up at the canopy above us, my mind churning with thoughts I could not voice.

After a long moment, he spoke, his voice a low murmur in the darkness. "I'm sorry," he said, his tone laced with something that sounded like regret. "I never wanted this to be... I never wanted to force this upon you."

I wanted to respond, to lash out, to tell him that his apologies meant nothing in the face of what had just passed between us. But my voice failed me, the words lodged in my throat like stones. Instead, I turned away, curling into myself, feeling the weight of his gaze on my back as he remained beside me, silent and watchful.

He eventually rose, dressing quietly, his movements careful and precise. I listened as he left the room, the door clicking softly behind him, leaving me alone in the vast, silent bed that felt colder than it had before.

As the days passed, the encounters continued, each one leaving me feeling more hollow, more resentful. Josiah kept his distance outside the bedroom, as though sensing my desire for solitude. But each night, he returned, his touch both familiar and foreign, a reminder of the duty we shared but never spoke of. I saw a flicker of sadness in his gaze each time, but he never said anything, never questioned my silence or my unwillingness to engage.

I could feel the bitterness growing within me, a resentment that spilled over into every aspect of my life here. I despised him for his patience, for his willingness to endure my coldness, for his refusal to confront the wall I had built between us. I despised the way he moved so easily between his roles as Duke and husband, as though our marriage were nothing more than another duty he fulfilled with careful precision.

And yet, beneath it all, there was a flicker of something else, a faint whisper of doubt that haunted me in the quiet moments. I couldn't deny that he was a dutiful man, that he carried out his responsibilities with a quiet dignity that should have impressed me. But that only deepened my resentment, for I wanted him to be different, wanted him to be as cold and indifferent as I had believed him to be. Instead, he was kind, patient, and relentless in his attempts to reach me, even when I gave him nothing in return.

In my heart, I knew that this bitterness, this anger, was as much my own as it was his. But I could not bring myself to let it go. I clung to it, letting it shield me from the vulnerability I feared, from the possibility that perhaps I had misjudged him, that perhaps this man who shared my bed was not the monster I had imagined him to be.

But until I could bear to face that truth, I would keep him at arm's length, buried beneath the weight of my own bitterness.

21

The Detached Duty

The chill in the room was unmistakable, even after the fire had been stoked. I'd heard that marriages of duty could feel detached, but I hadn't prepared myself for the cold wall of resentment that Jemima wore like armor. Every night felt like a penance, a reminder of how little warmth existed between us, how bound we were by obligation rather than choice.

The ritual was always the same—a silent, uncomfortable preparation for the night's duty. I could see the way her expression would harden as the evening approached, her eyes avoiding mine as Mary helped her prepare for bed. I would wait, the weight of expectation pressing down on me, knowing what was to come but dreading it all the same.

When I entered the room, the firelight flickering across the walls, Jemima lay stiffly beneath the covers, her gaze fixed resolutely on the canopy above. The tension between us was palpable, an invisible barrier that seemed to thicken with each passing night. I could feel her distaste radiating from her, her body rigid beneath me as I tried to fulfill my role with as much care and gentleness as I could muster. Her cold expression beneath me, the way her eyes seemed to stare past me as if I were not even there, cut deeper than any harsh words ever could.

I often hesitated before touching her, my hand hovering just above her skin as I tried to gauge whether she might soften, even just a little. But she never did. Her reluctance was plain, her body tense and unyielding, and each night became another reminder of the uncomfortable distance that stretched between us—a distance I couldn't seem to bridge, no matter how gentle I tried to be.

Part of me wanted to reassure her, to reach out and promise that I wouldn't ask anything of her she couldn't give. But the other part—the part that had grown weary of her glances of disdain, of the resentment that hardened her every movement—remained silent, determined not to make her burden any heavier. I knew how she saw me. And it was that knowledge, that constant awareness of her disappointment, that held me back from breaking the silence between us.

When the act was done, I would lie beside her, staring at the ceiling, the weight of her coldness pressing down on me. In those moments, I felt more alone than I ever had before, the emptiness of our marriage laid bare in the darkness of the room. I wanted to say something—anything—to ease the tension, to let her know that I wasn't the enemy she seemed to believe me to be. But the words always died on my tongue, swallowed by the heavy silence that filled the space between us.

In the aftermath, I often found myself lying awake beside her, watching the faint glow of the fire flicker across her face, wondering what thoughts ran through her mind. Did she hate me for this? For the role I was forced to play, for the intimacy that felt more like a transaction than anything resembling affection? I wondered if she felt as burdened by this expectation as I did, or if her disdain went even deeper, born of a belief that I was somehow to blame for all of it.

One night, unable to bear the silence any longer, I rose quietly from the bed, leaving her in the half-darkness. I walked to the library, hoping the solitude might offer some respite, some sense of peace in a life that had become a patchwork of expectations and disappointments.

The library was quiet, its shelves lined with volumes I hadn't had time to read. I sank into one of the leather chairs by the hearth, staring into the dim flames, the warmth barely touching the cold knot in my chest.

What had happened to us? To the hopeful beginnings I'd imagined, the fragile bond I'd once thought might grow between us? I felt foolish now, for believing that time or patience could bridge the gulf between us. Jemima's disdain seemed boundless, and every effort I made to treat her with kindness only seemed to deepen her resentment.

I ran a hand over my face, feeling the weariness that had settled into my bones. I had never sought this role, this life of endless scrutiny and inherited sins. But here I was, the Duke of Wellesley, husband to a woman who viewed me as little more than an unwanted obligation. And despite my efforts to honor both her and the title, I couldn't shake the feeling that I was failing, that every attempt I made was pushing her further away.

The next morning, I kept my distance, letting her go about her day without intrusion. I saw her briefly in the breakfast room, and the way she kept her gaze averted, the way her words were clipped and formal, only reminded me of how little I meant to her.

As I watched her leave, a dull ache settled in my chest, a quiet but relentless reminder that whatever connection I'd hoped to foster between us was slipping further out of reach with each passing day. If she saw me as unworthy, then perhaps I was.

22

A Growing Resentment

The doctor's voice was clear, cutting through the silence of the room with an unshakable certainty. "Congratulations, Your Grace," he said, his gaze shifting between Josiah and me with a practiced smile. "The Duchess is expecting."

The words hung in the air, heavy and final. Expecting. My hand instinctively moved to my abdomen, resting on the gentle curve that had begun to form there, a hollow motion, as if I were only just beginning to grasp the reality now confirmed. The slight swell of my belly had been a constant, silent reminder these past weeks, a change I had tried to ignore, to pretend wasn't real. I felt Josiah's gaze on me, and when I glanced at him, there was an unmistakable light in his eyes, a brightness that seemed almost... relieved.

He looked at me with a faint smile, his hand brushing against mine. "Jemima," he murmured, his voice soft with a warmth I'd rarely heard. "This is... it's wonderful news."

Wonderful? The word felt foreign, a label forced upon a feeling that was anything but wonderful. My body tensed, recoiling from his touch, and I could feel the walls closing in around me, the weight of duty tightening like a vise. I wanted to pull away, to shield myself from the expectations that seemed to press in from all sides.

The doctor carried on in a gentle, efficient manner, launching into instructions and advice in his matter-of-fact tone. I only half-listened, unable to focus on the details, too absorbed in my own thoughts, my own private sense of dread.

...plenty of rest, minimal exertion," he was saying, his voice fading in and out of focus. "Your Grace, I'll recommend a daily tonic to support her constitution. And as we approach the coming months, I'll return to check on her regularly."

The examination itself had been brief; he'd checked my pulse, felt my growing abdomen, taken a vial of my urine to test. It was all so orderly, so predictable, the entire process no more personal than a routine visit for a seasonal ailment. Yet his words—his confirmation—seared into my mind, a mark that I couldn't erase.

I heard Josiah's voice distantly as he thanked the doctor, his tone formal but soft. They exchanged words that I couldn't quite grasp, words of congratulation and plans for future appointments. My mind was elsewhere, spiraling as I grappled with the reality of what had just been confirmed.

Pregnant. I was carrying Josiah's child. I should be happy that I'm finally carrying a successor. If I give birth to a baby boy then my son will be the future duke even if Josiah has an illegitimate child.

I should have been relieved that I was finally pregnant too after those long nights. Nights where Josiah and I spent time having intercourse. With my pregnancy I wouldn't have to sleep in his arms every night.

But, why did I feel upset and unhappy about this pregnancy?

I don't know where this feeling of resentment came from. Maybe because I didn't expect to carry Josiah's child in my belly so soon. And the feeling of resentment was made worse because in my heart, I still tried to imagine it was Simon's. The thought that this might have been Simon's child instead brought a fleeting sense of what might have been—a life filled with warmth rather than obligation. Yet, the reality persisted, no matter how many times it echoed in my mind, refusing to settle.

When the doctor finally left, Josiah turned to me, his expression a mixture of tenderness and gratitude. "Jemima," he began, reaching for my hand. "I know... I know this has been difficult, and I haven't made it easy. But this child... it's a new beginning."

A new beginning? The words twisted inside me, filling me with an unbidden anger. This wasn't a beginning; it was the end. The end of any semblance of freedom, the end of my hope for a life that was truly my own. This child—this symbol of duty and expectation—was nothing more than a reminder of the prison I had found myself in, bound to a man I could barely stand, carrying a legacy I wanted no part of. And beneath that anger, a darker suspicion festered—Josiah's polite detachment, his careful distance, felt like a mask for something else. Was he hiding infidelities behind that calm exterior? Or Does he really just think of me as a pawn to give him an heir then he seek comfort elsewhere, knowing I was here, trapped by duty? The thought fed my resentment, a growing certainty that made his every gesture feel hollow and insincere.

I pulled my hand from his, the movement subtle but deliberate, my gaze fixed on the floor. "If you'll excuse me," I muttered, barely able to keep the resentment from seeping into my voice. Without waiting for his reply, I turned and left the room, my footsteps echoing through the hall as I retreated to the sanctuary of my own chambers.

Once alone, the emotions I had held in check came flooding over me, crashing through the barriers I'd so carefully constructed. Resentment, bitterness, even a dark edge of loathing. I pressed my hand to my swollen abdomen, feeling the faint roundness beneath my fingertips, and a wave of revulsion swept over me.

This child... this child was a reminder of everything I had been forced to endure, of the cold, detached duty that defined my marriage, of the intimacy that had been demanded of me with no regard for my own desires. How was I to love a life that had been created not out of affection, but out of obligation? How was I to cherish a child that would forever tie me to a man I could not bring myself to forgive?

Days turned into weeks, and with each passing moment, my resentment grew, festering within me like a wound that refused to heal. I felt trapped, suffocated by the constant reminders of my role as Duchess, by the expectations of everyone around me. Everywhere I went, I could feel the household's gaze upon me, the subtle glances, the whispers that carried through the halls.

They knew, all of them, and they were watching, waiting for the heir I was now expected to bear.

My body had begun to change, the swell of my belly becoming more pronounced, an undeniable sign of the life growing within me. I tried to deny it, to ignore the physical changes that were becoming increasingly difficult to hide. The curve of my belly was no longer something I could dismiss, a visible manifestation of Josiah's child growing inside me. The roundness made my clothes tighter, my movements slower, and it was impossible not to feel the weight of it, the constant reminder of what had taken root within me. I avoided Josiah as much as possible, retreating to my chambers, finding solace in solitude. When we did cross paths, I kept my responses curt, my tone cold, determined to shut him out, to protect myself from the forced intimacy that had brought me to this place. I told myself that he cared only for the legacy, that this child was little more than a necessary addition to his title and estate. I could see the faint shadow of hurt in his eyes, the way his gaze softened when he looked at me, as if he wanted to bridge the gap between us. But I refused to let him. He'd had his chance, and he'd used me to fulfill his duty, nothing more.

The resentment grew, dark and unyielding, filling the empty spaces within me. I began to contemplate ways to rid myself of this burden, thoughts that I dared not voice, even to myself. I knew, deep down, that such thoughts were dangerous, that they went against everything I had been taught, everything society expected of me. But I couldn't deny the fierce desire to escape, to find some way to reclaim the freedom that had been taken from me.

And yet, there was no escape. No way out of this life, no way to undo what had been done. I was trapped, bound to a future I had never chosen, carrying a child I had no desire to bring into the world. The bitterness settled in my heart, hardening with each passing day, until it felt as though it had become a part of me, woven into the very fabric of my being.

I could feel the child growing within me, a subtle presence that served only to deepen my resentment. Each movement, each faint flutter, was a reminder of the life that I now carried, a life that bound me irrevocably to Josiah, to the title, to the duty that I had never wanted.

And as I sat alone in the dim silence of my chambers, I wondered how long I could endure this life, this bitterness that had taken root within me. I wondered if there was any way to escape, or if I was destined to spend the rest of my days as little more than a vessel, a symbol, a Duchess bound by duty and obligation.

I pressed a hand to my abdomen, feeling the faint stirrings beneath my fingers, and for the first time, I allowed myself to acknowledge the depth of my own loathing. In a moment of desperation, I pressed harder, as if somehow I could will the child away, make it disappear. But the pressure only brought pain, a sharp reminder of how real this was, how inescapable. This child, this life, was a prison, and I was its unwilling captive.

And though I knew that such thoughts were dangerous, that they were thoughts a mother should never harbor, I could not bring myself to care.

23

More than just Duty

The days after Jemima's pregnancy was confirmed seemed to shift the very air within Wellesley Manor. I could feel her growing distance like an invisible wall between us, her gaze turned inward, guarded and impenetrable. She retreated more and more, her silences stretching longer, her responses to me clipped and formal. And as much as I respected her need for space, I could not ignore the subtle signs of her struggle, the weariness that shadowed her eyes, the tension in her posture.

More than anything, I wanted to reach out to her, to share in this moment that should have been a source of joy. I wanted to place my hand on her growing belly, to feel the faint stirrings of the life we had created, to speak softly to the baby—our baby. There were times when I would catch a glimpse of her, her hand resting unconsciously on her abdomen, and I felt a deep, almost primal urge to join her, to lay my hand there beside hers and tell our child about the world that awaited them. I imagined reading stories to her belly, connecting with the baby even before they took their first breath. But Jemima's cold demeanor made it clear that such intimacy was unwelcome. She was unapproachable, her resentment palpable, and the last thing I wanted was to make her feel pressured or invaded.

So, I tried other ways to show her I cared. It began with small notes—simple, quiet things. I knew she enjoyed poetry, so I'd scribble a line or two of verse on fine parchment and leave it tucked on her breakfast tray or by her favorite chair in the library. I chose lines that might remind her of beauty, of gentleness, something that might counter the weight she seemed to carry.

"A gentle reminder, to ease your day: beauty surrounds us if we dare to look," I wrote in one, slipping it between the pages of the book she was currently reading. I hoped she might see it as a gesture of understanding, that even if I could not reach her through words, perhaps I could reach her through these quiet symbols of thoughtfulness.

Then there was the matter of food. She'd barely eaten during the gatherings, and I had noticed that her appetite had dwindled since. I arranged with the cook to prepare some of her favorites, dishes I'd learned she enjoyed: warm bread with lavender honey, fresh fruits, delicate soups that would not weigh too heavily. I knew pregnancy could be exhausting, that her body required nourishment more than ever, and it felt right to try to help her, even in this small way.

Occasionally, I'd send Mary, her maid, to her with a soft shawl if the evening turned chilly or a soothing tonic I'd had the doctor recommend for her well-being. The gestures were small, unobtrusive, and I hoped, comforting. I had learned, by now, that anything grand or overtly affectionate might only push her further away. These subtle acts, however, felt safer—quiet reminders that I was here, that I cared, that she was not alone in this.

But despite my careful efforts, I saw no hint of appreciation from her. When I left a note or had a favorite dish sent to her, I'd hear nothing in response. She would eat sparingly, not meeting my gaze, dismissing these gestures as if they meant nothing. Once, I passed her in the corridor just after Mary had brought her a fresh bouquet of garden roses—her favorites, or so I'd thought—and she barely glanced at it, her expression one of faint distaste.

And still, I tried.

One evening, I penned a note, unsure if she would even read it, but needing to convey some semblance of care, however muted. "If there is anything you need, anything that might ease your days, please know that you need only ask." I left it on the tea tray outside her chambers, not wanting to impose, only to offer.

But when I saw her the next morning, her gaze was colder than ever, as though my words had only deepened her bitterness. She moved past me without a word, her shoulders squared, her expression unreadable, and I felt the ache of my own helplessness settle like a stone in my chest.

It was in that moment that I realized something, a painful truth that I hadn't fully grasped before. Jemima viewed my actions as mere duty, as obligations that meant nothing beyond the surface, that my concern for her was only another performance in this marriage of necessity. She believed that every gesture was calculated, insincere, nothing more than a reflection of the role I was supposed to play. And no matter what I did, no matter how quiet, how genuine my attempts, I would always be seen through the lens of her resentment.

I'd hoped that these acts, however subtle, might begin to show her that I cared, that I wanted more than duty between us. But each attempt seemed to draw her further away, hardening the wall between us rather than bridging it. She saw only obligation where I had tried to show care, saw duty where I had meant kindness.

I wasn't sure what else I could do. Confronting her, demanding to know why she kept herself so distant, felt impossible. I feared it would only deepen the wound, confirm to her that my intentions were selfish, that I only sought her gratitude to ease my own guilt. And yet, I could not simply do nothing. To stand by, to watch her suffer without offering anything, felt wrong in a way I could not ignore.

So I continued, silently, hoping that, in time, these gestures might reach her, that she might one day see them as something more than duty. And perhaps, as the weeks passed, as the baby grew, she might come to understand that my actions were not just for her role as Duchess, but for Jemima herself, the woman behind the title.

I watched her belly grow, the undeniable curve of pregnancy making itself known beneath her dresses. I wanted so badly to touch it, to lay my hand gently on that growing swell and feel the life we had created. I wanted to connect, to show her that this child was not just a duty, but a part of both of us. But Jemima remained unapproachable, her coldness a barrier I dared not cross. I respected her need for distance, but it pained me all the same—to be so close, yet so impossibly far from the life growing within her, from the woman carrying it.

And yet, I kept trying. For all I had was the hope that maybe, one day, she might come to see that she was more than duty to me.

24

Unexpected Softness

I was twelve weeks along now, and it showed. I couldn't ignore the gentle curve of my belly, round and unmistakable, reminding me with each glance in the mirror that the child Josiah and I had created was real, growing stronger with each passing day. My dresses had begun to tighten, and I could feel the subtle pressure of the baby against the fabric. Every morning, I noticed the changes—the slight roundness that became impossible to hide, the shift in my center of gravity. There was no more pretending, no more denial. The child was here, and with it came an undeniable presence, a quiet force that demanded acknowledgment.

It was strange, this mix of emotions that settled within me as I noticed Josiah's small acts of care. For weeks, I'd pushed his gestures aside, dismissing them as mere duty, gifts intended only to maintain appearances. And yet, with every little token he sent—a silk scarf to keep me warm on brisk mornings, a lavender-scented pillow that somehow eased my restless nights—I began to feel... something. Not the bitter resentment I'd once clung to, but a quiet, reluctant appreciation.

I had begun keeping some of the small notes he left for me, tucking them away in a drawer without allowing myself to read them more than once. They were simple, unobtrusive words of encouragement, and yet I found myself drawn to them, re-reading lines like "I hope this helps you feel at ease," or "Take heart; you're not alone in this." The notes, with their understated tenderness, had begun to touch something within me, something that I hadn't realized was yearning for acknowledgment. A part of me still resisted, still tried to convince myself that these gestures were nothing more than his attempt to fulfill his duty. But another part of me—a small, growing part—wondered if there might be more.

The doctor had visited again that afternoon, his usual instruments spread out on the table. Josiah stood beside me, close enough that I could feel his presence without needing to look at him. He'd always come for the doctor's appointments, listening intently to every piece of advice, every word of encouragement. His presence, though silent, was steady, and I found myself strangely comforted by it, even as I tried to ignore the warmth of his proximity.

"Her Grace is progressing well," the doctor said, his tone soothing. He turned to me, offering a small smile. "You have a strong, healthy baby. That much is clear."

I nodded, keeping my expression calm, though there was something about those words—a strong, healthy baby—that stirred a faint feeling of relief within me. The child was growing, thriving. And despite the confusion and fear that lingered, I couldn't help but feel a small, reluctant sense of hope.

But Josiah wasn't so easily reassured. "Are you sure?" he asked, glancing from me to the doctor with a faint crease of worry on his brow. "Her belly seems... well, it's quite large, isn't it? Is that... is that normal?"

I found myself glancing up at him, surprised by the concern in his voice. He looked down at me, and for a moment, our eyes met, his gaze filled with something I couldn't quite name. Worry, certainly, but also a gentleness that made my chest ache in a way I hadn't expected. In that fleeting moment, I realized that he truly cared, that his concern was not just for the title or the legacy, but for me—for the child we were bringing into this world together.

The doctor chuckled, shaking his head. "Quite normal, Your Grace. Every woman carries differently, but I assure you, this is a very good sign. The Duchess should continue with gentle walks and, of course, ample rest. It will help make labor easier."

Josiah nodded slowly, his shoulders relaxing as he absorbed the doctor's words. His hand brushed against mine for the briefest moment before he drew it back, as if catching himself. I felt a strange warmth spread through me, an unbidden softness that made me feel lighter, if only for a heartbeat. The tension that had held me rigid seemed to ease, if only slightly, and I found myself wondering what it might be like to truly let him in.

"Thank you, Doctor," Josiah said quietly, his tone steady but undeniably relieved.

After the doctor left, there was a lingering quiet in the room, the kind of silence that held its own weight. Josiah cleared his throat, glancing toward the window. "If... if you'd like," he began, his voice hesitant, "I could join you on your walks. Only if you wish it, of course. I understand if... if you'd prefer to go alone."

The offer was so unexpected that it caught me off guard, and I looked up at him, surprised by the softness in his expression, the way he seemed almost vulnerable, as if he were offering me something fragile. For the first time, I sensed that his concern was genuine, that his care for me was not just an extension of duty, but something deeper, something... personal.

"I... I think I might like that," I replied, the words slipping out before I could stop them.

His face softened, and for a fleeting moment, I thought I saw the faintest hint of a smile in his eyes. It was a look I hadn't seen before, something quiet and unguarded that made my pulse quicken, though I couldn't explain why.

The next morning, we walked together through the gardens, our steps slow and measured, the air around us cool and fresh. Josiah kept a respectful distance, his hands clasped behind his back, and yet I could feel his presence beside me, steady and solid, a comforting warmth that I hadn't anticipated. The gentle weight of my belly swayed with each step, a physical reminder of the life growing inside me. And for the first time, I didn't resent it. I placed my hand on the curve of my stomach, feeling the gentle swell beneath my fingers, and there was something almost peaceful about it.

The early sunlight filtered through the trees, casting dappled shadows across the path, and for a moment, it felt as though the tension between us had lifted, like a mist finally giving way to sunlight. Josiah walked beside me in silence, and yet, somehow, it didn't feel uncomfortable. It felt... peaceful.

After a while, he spoke, his tone soft. "Do you feel well, Jemima? Truly?"

There was an earnestness in his voice that surprised me, and I found myself nodding. "Yes. More so, I think, than I expected."

He looked down, a thoughtful expression crossing his face. "I'm glad to hear it. I only want... that is, I hope this journey becomes easier for you, somehow."

The words were simple, but they stayed with me, lingering long after our walk had ended. His gestures, his presence, his quiet concern—all of it was beginning to weave itself into the walls I'd built around my heart, chipping away at my bitterness, even if I wasn't quite ready to admit it.

Later that evening, I sat in my room, my hands resting on my belly, feeling the faint stirrings within. There was a quietness inside me that hadn't been there before, a softening that I couldn't explain but also couldn't deny. I didn't know if it was the baby or Josiah or simply the passing of time, but I felt... different. Lighter, somehow, as if some part of me had begun to let go of the resentment I'd carried for so long.

I still felt wary, still hesitant to let my guard down entirely. But I couldn't deny that something had changed, that the bitterness I'd once felt so fiercely was beginning to fade, replaced by a quiet, reluctant warmth that crept in like the morning sun.

For the first time, I allowed myself to wonder if perhaps, one day, I might truly come to trust him—and even come to find comfort in his presence, to let go of Simon's shadow and fully embrace the life I now had before me.

25

The Things I didn't Realize Before

It was as if I were seeing him for the first time. Or, perhaps, I was finally allowing myself to look.

Josiah had taken to walking with me each morning, as the doctor had recommended. In the beginning, our outings were formal, almost stilted, with little more than pleasantries exchanged between us. But over the past few weeks, I had noticed the smallest gestures—gestures that, despite myself, made me feel oddly... cared for.

One morning, after an unexpectedly strong wave of nausea had sent me rushing from the breakfast table, I had hardly made it out of the dining room before Josiah was at my side. When I finally emerged from the washroom, pale and exhausted, I found him waiting in the hallway, his brow furrowed with concern.

Without a word, he offered me his arm, and as I leaned on him, he guided me back to my chambers with the same gentleness he'd shown me during our walks. I expected him to leave once I was safely inside, but instead, he took up a cloth and, with the faintest hint of awkwardness, dabbed at the corners of my mouth. His hand trembled slightly, his expression one of focused concentration, as though wiping my face was a delicate task he dared not fumble.

It was an odd, clumsy act of care—and yet, it touched something within me. The sight of this man, usually so composed and self-assured, handling me with such earnestness, made me want to laugh and sigh all at once.

"Thank you," I murmured, unsure of what else to say.

Josiah merely nodded, his gaze averted, a hint of color rising to his cheeks as he quickly stepped back, as if giving me space was the only way to keep from embarrassing us both further.

I watched him leave, his back straight, his hands clasped behind him as he walked down the hallway. There was a small smile tugging at the corner of my lips. And when I looked down at the small cloth he'd left behind, I found myself holding it, unable to dismiss the gesture as easily as I once might have.

But it wasn't just in those small moments of care. As our walks continued, I began to see other things about him—little things, details I'd once dismissed. There was a certain gentleness to his manner, especially when he thought no one was watching. I'd caught him watching the birds in the garden more than once, his gaze thoughtful, a faint smile on his lips. His presence, so steady and reassuring, had begun to feel... familiar, a warmth I could no longer ignore.

One afternoon, as I struggled to sit up after a particularly restless nap, Josiah entered without warning. Seeing me in discomfort, he crossed the room quickly, his hands slipping under my arms as he lifted me with an ease that startled me. I felt his strength, the solidness of his frame, and for a moment, I found myself glancing up at him, surprised by the warmth in his gaze, the gentle but unwavering support he offered without a single word of judgment.

He chuckled softly as he set me back down, the sound rumbling low in his chest. And for the first time, I found myself truly *seeing* him.

It struck me then, just how handsome he was—handsome in a way I hadn't allowed myself to acknowledge before. His features were strong, more defined than Simon's ever were, his jawline sharper, his cheekbones high and finely cut. His eyes, a shade of blue that seemed to soften in the sunlight, held a warmth that made them almost... endearing. And when he laughed, showing just a hint of his teeth, it was like watching a boyish charm emerge from a man who was otherwise so reserved.

I hadn't noticed these things before, perhaps because I'd been so determined not to notice. But now that I'd allowed myself even the smallest glimpse, I couldn't ignore it. His handsomeness was not the polished charm I'd known with Simon. No, Josiah's appeal lay in the quiet way he moved through his duties, the way he managed both strength and gentleness, all without expectation.

Another morning, when the nausea hit me harder than usual, I hadn't even reached the washroom before my legs gave way. Josiah, who must have heard my stumbling footsteps, appeared almost instantly, catching me before I could fall. He scooped me up as though I weighed nothing at all, his arms steady, his expression focused as he carried me back to my chambers.

There was a tenderness in his touch, something almost protective, that made my breath catch. As he lowered me onto the bed, his hand brushed against mine, his thumb lingering for just a second before he pulled away, his face flushed as he turned to leave.

"I'll send for a tonic," he said softly, not meeting my gaze.

It would have been easy to say nothing, to let him leave, but I found myself reaching out, my fingers catching his sleeve. "Josiah," I whispered, unsure what had come over me.

He stopped, his expression one of surprise as he turned back to me. I hadn't prepared any words, had no reason to keep him there except that, in that moment, I didn't want him to go. His presence, his touch, the quiet care he'd shown me—some part of me, some part I had buried deep, wanted him to stay.

"Thank you," I said finally, my voice barely above a whisper. It was a simple phrase, but I hoped he would understand that it meant more than gratitude for his kindness. It was an acknowledgment, a reluctant recognition of the man he was, a man I was only now beginning to see.

His gaze softened, his lips curving into the faintest smile. "It's my pleasure, Jemima," he replied, his voice warm, sincere.

As he left, I felt a warmth settle over me, a feeling I couldn't quite name but didn't entirely want to push away. And for the first time since our marriage, I felt a flicker of something that wasn't resentment, something softer, something that felt strangely like hope.

26

A New Light

As the days slipped into one another, I found myself thinking of Josiah more often, my thoughts lingering on his kindness, his gentleness, the way he always seemed to appear just when I needed him most. He was attuned to my every discomfort, my every unspoken need, without making me feel as though he expected anything in return. There was no obligation, no sense of duty in his eyes—just a quiet, genuine offering of support that felt like warmth in the coldest moments.

I found myself searching for him during our morning walks, waiting to catch the small quirks in his expression that I had come to recognize. His glances had grown softer, lingering in ways that made my heart flutter unsteadily in my chest. When he walked beside me in silence, I no longer felt the urge to fill the quiet with trivial chatter. There was a peace in that silence, a gentle understanding that made me feel safe in a way I hadn't known before.

One evening, as I sat in the drawing room with a book open in my lap, I heard the familiar rhythm of his footsteps approaching. He paused in the doorway, hesitating for a moment as though unsure whether he should enter. Our eyes met, and before I could stop myself, I offered him a small smile—a wordless invitation that seemed to ease the tension in his shoulders.

He entered the room, his movements slow and careful, taking a seat across from me. He didn't speak, but his presence filled the space between us, a quiet warmth that was comforting rather than imposing. I turned my attention back to my book, yet my focus stayed on him, aware of the comforting weight of his gaze on me.

It dawned on me then, how little I had allowed myself to truly look at Josiah—to see him for who he was, beyond Simon's shadow, beyond the man bound to me by circumstances beyond our control. He had been patient, always waiting in the wings, never pushing or demanding more from me than I could give. In his silence, he had granted me the freedom to find my own way to him, a gift I hadn't realized I needed until now.

I glanced at him over the edge of my book, noticing the thoughtful expression in his eyes, the faint smile that softened his features. There was a strength to Josiah that didn't need words—it was in the way he cared for others, in his quiet gestures that spoke of a love far deeper than mere duty. Simon had been charming, effortlessly so, but Josiah was something else entirely. He was real, grounded, and steady in a way I hadn't known I needed.

The thought startled me, the realization coming out of nowhere, but I couldn't ignore it. For the first time, I felt the ghost of Simon fading—not disappearing entirely, but losing its grip on my heart. The bitterness I had carried with me for so long began to slip away, replaced by a sense of acceptance. Simon was gone, a part of my past that no longer held me captive. And here was Josiah, waiting patiently, offering a future I hadn't thought possible.

As if sensing my thoughts, Josiah looked up, his gaze meeting mine. His eyes were soft, a gentleness in them that drew me in, inviting me to open a door I had kept firmly shut.

"Jemima," he said quietly, his voice warm and sincere. "You seem... different tonight."

I hesitated, searching for the right words, unsure if I could truly express what I felt. But the words came, unbidden and honest. "I think I'm finally beginning to see things clearly," I replied, my voice soft but certain.

He held my gaze, his expression calm, waiting. There was no pressure, no expectation—just the quiet patience that had always defined him. Josiah, who had borne the weight of Simon's mistakes, who had faced whispers and rumors without once defending himself, who had given me the space to find my own path.

"Thank you," I whispered, the simple phrase carrying a depth I hoped he could hear. It wasn't just gratitude—it was an acknowledgment, a release, a promise that I was ready to leave the shadows behind and step into the light with him.

A gentle smile touched his lips, one that reached his eyes, warming them with a softness that made my heart swell. "It's been my pleasure, Jemima. Truly."

He rose from his seat, moving to kneel beside me, his eyes never leaving mine. His hand found mine, his fingers brushing over my knuckles in a tender caress. I felt my heart stutter in my chest, a rush of warmth spreading through me, an emotion I hadn't dared to name until now.

"Jemima," he murmured, his voice trembling slightly, filled with emotions too vast to be contained by words. "You seem... at peace tonight. It's different, and I can't help but notice."

I hesitated for a moment, then gave a small nod. "I think I am finding some peace," I replied softly. "Thanks to you, Josiah. For everything you've done, for being here without asking for anything in return."

His eyes softened, and he reached out, taking my hand gently in his. "It's been my pleasure, Jemima. Truly."

The sincerity in his words filled the room, and I felt my heart swell, warmth spreading through me. I knew that whatever had kept us apart before was now dissolving, leaving room for something new, something real between us.

His eyes glistened with emotion, and he leaned in, pressing his lips gently to mine. The kiss was soft, tender, filled with the promise of a future we would build together—a future built not on duty or obligation, but on love, trust, and mutual respect.

When we finally pulled apart, he rested his forehead against mine, his breath mingling with mine as we stayed close, savoring the moment. I looked into his eyes, seeing the love there, seeing the man who had always been by my side, who had never given up on me, even when I had given up on myself.

"We'll make this work," I said, my voice filled with certainty. "Together."

He nodded, his smile widening, his fingers brushing a stray tear from my cheek. "Together," he echoed, his voice filled with warmth and hope.

A weight seemed to lift from the room, the tension that had kept us apart easing just enough for me to feel a flicker of hope. I knew it wouldn't be easy, that the past would not simply fade away, but for the first time, it felt as though we were both willing to take that step—together.

"Thank you, Jemima," he murmured. "For giving this a chance."

I gave a small nod. "I suppose it's time I stopped running from what's inevitable.

In that moment, the past was behind us, and all that remained was the future—one we would create together, hand in hand, heart to heart. I knew that whatever lay ahead, we were ready to face it, bound by a love that was stronger than any storm, a love that had grown quietly but fiercely, enduring and true.

27

From Duty to Desire

The pile of correspondence on my desk seemed endless tonight, a mountain of estate matters, tenant requests, and ledgers that demanded my attention. I had planned to finish early, yet every line blurred as I fought off fatigue. My temples throbbed, and I brought a hand to my forehead, massaging gently, wishing I could simply leave it all and see Jemima.

Jemima. The thought of her sent a warmth through me, one that softened the edges of the day's frustrations. She had stopped calling me "Your Grace" so often, and each time I heard her say "Josiah," my heart beat faster, the distance between us closing ever so slightly. For so long, I'd hoped she might see me as something more than just the man she'd been duty-bound to marry. And now, each glance, each touch, and each gentle smile she offered seemed to be an answer to that silent prayer.

A knock at the door broke my reverie, and I called out, "Come in."

The door opened to reveal Jemima, holding a small plate in her hands, her gaze warm and affectionate. The faintest of smiles played on her lips, and I couldn't help but mirror it, feeling the day's tension ease away.

"Jemima," I said, trying to keep the surprise from my voice. "Is there something you need?"

Her smile widened, and she held up the plate. "I thought you might like some freshly baked pastries. I know you've been working late..."

I felt my heart soften further, her small gesture somehow carrying more meaning than words could ever convey. She was here, bringing me something as simple as pastries, yet it felt like so much more—a willingness to share her presence, to let me into her thoughts, however quietly.

"Oh, just leave them there," I said, indicating a side table, my words betraying the reluctance I felt to keep her from my space. "I'll have them in a little while."

But instead of setting them down and leaving, Jemima stepped fully into the room, crossing the distance to place the plate on the edge of my desk, her eyes fixed on me with an intent curiosity.

"Are you very busy, Josiah?" Her voice was soft, her eyes sincere, and the sound of my name—so rarely spoken by her—was a balm, a melody that made the walls around me fade away.

"Yes," I replied, giving her a weary smile. "Unfortunately, tonight seems to have a way of reminding me that the work never truly ends."

She glanced at the piles of parchment, her eyes sympathetic, then looked back at me, a small, mischievous glint dancing in her gaze. "Perhaps," she murmured, a gentle determination in her tone, "you might allow me to help you in some small way?"

I raised an eyebrow, curiosity piqued. "And how would you manage that, my dear?"

A slight blush colored her cheeks, yet she held my gaze steadily. "Well… if it wouldn't be too improper, I could… feed you?" Her voice softened, and I caught a hint of nervousness beneath her boldness, an innocence that made me smile.

I blinked, surprised by her offer, then felt a warmth that spread from my chest to every part of me, the humor of it too tempting to resist. "Only if," I murmured, leaning a little closer, "it comes with an exchange of kisses."

Her eyes widened, then softened, and she nodded, her voice barely a whisper. "I think that can be arranged."

Without another word, I drew her close, pressing my lips to hers. The kiss began as a gentle meeting, but it deepened quickly, a stirring passion emerging that had long been waiting. Her lips were soft, inviting, and the warmth between us ignited into a quiet, smoldering intensity.

Before I knew it, she had eased into my lap, her arms draping around my neck as she returned each kiss with a fervor that surprised us both. There, by my desk, with the reports and ledgers strewn about us, the weight of duty melted away, leaving only the two of us, our world narrowing to the space we shared.

I let my hand rest on her belly, feeling its firm curve beneath my fingers. Her body was changing, softening in new ways that I hadn't dared to dwell on before, and yet now, touching her like this, I felt nothing but reverence for the life we had created, the child growing beneath her heart. It was a marvel, an unspoken promise, a bond that would forever tie us together, and at this moment, it felt as natural as breathing.

"Josiah," she whispered, her hand finding mine and pressing it gently against her stomach. "I... I didn't realize it could be like this." Her gaze was vulnerable, her voice trembling with a mixture of wonder and hesitation.

"Neither did I," I replied, my voice thick with emotion, with the gratitude I felt for this chance to share something deeper with her. "But I can't imagine it any other way."

She gave a small laugh, her eyes shining. "I'd wondered... if you'd even wanted this at all, or if it was only because it was expected."

Her words struck me, the sorrow in them clear, and I reached up to cradle her face, brushing my thumb across her cheek. "I want this, Jemima. I want you, and I want our child." My voice softened, a whisper just for her. "This isn't duty. This is... it's everything."

She closed her eyes, leaning into my touch, and for the first time, I felt the walls between us crumble, the spaces that had kept us apart dissolving into something soft and safe. I held her close, my lips finding hers again, and as we kissed, the future opened before us, bright with possibility, grounded in a love that felt unshakeable.

We stayed like that for a long while, wrapped in each other, the world beyond forgotten. Whatever challenges lay ahead, I knew we would face them together, bound not by duty but by choice. And that knowledge, that precious certainty, filled me with a joy I hadn't thought possible, a hope that I would hold onto, no matter what awaited us.

28

A Spark of Betrayal

The crowded ballroom was alive with laughter and music, the air thick with the hum of gossip, and the sharp scent of perfume that lingered like a quiet warning. I drifted from one group to the next, forcing polite smiles and nods, all while my mind was elsewhere. A fortnight ago, I would have passed through this crowd with a detached indifference, immune to their whispers. But tonight, something had changed. Josiah's care had, against all logic, stirred a warmth I hadn't expected—so much so that even his absence tonight felt oddly painful.

The very thought made me angry, as though I were betraying my own heart with feelings I'd sworn never to entertain. And yet, the warmth lingered. I hadn't seen him since he'd helped me through a particularly bad bout of nausea that morning, his hands steady as he'd held me, his touch gentle as he wiped my brow and helped me back to bed. The memory was still fresh, and I could hardly deny the confusion it brought me.

And then I heard it.

Two ladies, dressed in vibrant gowns with plumed feathers perched atop their heads, were tucked away near the corner, their voices lowered to what they surely thought was a whisper.

"Well, of course she's just a replacement," one of them said, her voice tinged with derision. "A tragic accident, the poor Duke left to clean up the mess. It's only fitting he'd marry her to save her reputation—and now, of course, the heir will cement her place."

Her friend giggled, nodding enthusiastically. "Indeed. But even with an heir on the way, he only cares for family honor. Why, it's whispered that he has an illegitimate child hidden away somewhere—imagine the scandal! Oh, he's clever, I'll grant him that. Behind that charming smile, he's managed to keep every sordid affair out of sight."

A chill crept down my spine as their words sank in. The image they painted—the idea that Josiah's politeness was little more than a carefully constructed mask, hiding infidelities and indiscretions—stirred something dark and bitter within me. I had known of these rumors before our marriage, of course. I'd brushed them off with cold indifference, assuming that if he were to stray, I would hardly care.

But now, after all these weeks, after the softness he'd shown, the gentle touches, the quiet walks—I found myself furious. If this were true, if he were truly keeping a mistress while lavishing polite attention on me, then he was the worst kind of hypocrite. His kindness, his gentle touch, his care—they would all be lies. And I felt my heart sink at the very thought.

The second woman leaned closer to her friend, her voice lowering to a conspiratorial whisper. "Can you imagine the patience it takes to entertain her? He probably stays at her side purely for appearances. It's not as if he could have refused, after all. He was just left with the mess his brother made."

Her words struck me like a slap, a reminder of the position I'd been forced into. Yes, Josiah had inherited this marriage, just as he'd inherited the dukedom. And though he had shown me kindness, I couldn't help but wonder if they were right—if he merely saw me as a duty, a pawn to cement his family's legacy.

A surge of anger rose within me. It was bad enough that he would play this polite, caring husband while I struggled with my resentment and bitterness. But to think that he might have a secret life, a hidden lover somewhere, all while keeping me here, bound to a future I hadn't chosen, made my stomach churn with rage.

My fingers tightened around the stem of my glass, the coolness of it grounding me as I struggled to keep my expression calm, my gaze fixed ahead, even as my mind whirled with their words. It shouldn't bother me, I told myself. After all, I didn't love him. I had never wanted this marriage; I had never asked for his affection. And yet, when I thought of the small moments we'd shared, the quiet tenderness he'd shown, the glimmers of hope I hadn't allowed myself to fully admit... something inside me twisted, a betrayal so sharp that I could barely breathe.

I hated myself for caring. I hated the baby, hated the life it would bind me to, hated that Josiah's soft looks and fleeting touches had begun to weaken my resolve. I wanted to turn back, to lock myself away, to purge this growing affection before it ruined me completely.

But when I thought of him—his careful way of tending to me, the way he'd looked at me with such genuine worry just that morning—I felt my anger flare again, tangled with confusion and something dangerously close to jealousy.

The women's voices faded, and I found myself alone, surrounded by the sea of gowns and laughter, feeling as though I had been cast adrift. The small flickers of warmth I'd begun to feel for Josiah now felt foolish, like some naive hope I'd clung to without even realizing it. I took a deep breath, willing myself to calm, to remember that this was a marriage of duty, that his gestures were likely nothing more than a reflection of that duty.

And yet, I couldn't shake the feeling of betrayal, the sense that he had somehow wronged me without even knowing it.

With my hand resting on my belly, I left the ballroom, barely aware of the polite nods and greetings cast my way. I wanted to be alone, to banish these thoughts, to forget the glimmers of warmth that had slipped into my heart.

Back in my chambers, I sat by the window, staring out into the darkened garden, the moon casting a pale glow over the grounds. I wanted to be free of these feelings, free of the resentment and jealousy that simmered just beneath the surface. I pressed a hand to my belly, feeling the faint roundness beneath my fingertips, and I felt the weight of everything settling over me—the marriage, the rumors, the child that bound me to this life.

I told myself that I shouldn't care, that it didn't matter if he had secrets, if he cared for someone else. And yet, each time I pictured his gentle smile, his rare, genuine laugh, each memory only served to deepen my anger and confusion.

For perhaps the first time, I acknowledged the truth: I wanted more from him. And that, more than anything else, terrified me.

29

A Desperate Rejection

The gossip and whispers of the woman in the ballroom were still ringing in my head. I didn't want to get distracted because everything they said was true. But, I couldn't stop myself from feeling strange creeping in. Disappointment, hurt, even rejection of the feelings that arose. I bit my lip, I shouldn't be hurt, right?

Didn't I already know that our marriage was just a transaction. That Josiah married me for the sake of our family relationship. And I already knew that Josiah married me to settle things after Simon died. But, why am I disappointed? Is it because I expected Josiah to marry me because he was saving my uncertain future after Simon died?

And now Josiah's baby is growing inside me. No matter what reason Josiah had for marrying me or whether our marriage was forced, I was still carrying his child. That's a reality that can't be changed.

I already knew that I was just an instrument to carry and give birth to Josiah's successor. But, I was lulled by his sweet gestures and attention. I'd gotten over feeling upset about being pregnant and about to give birth to a baby I didn't even fully want.

I pressed a hand to my belly, feeling the slight but undeniable swell beneath my fingertips. It was real. This child, this consequence of a marriage I hadn't chosen, was real and growing, and I couldn't ignore it any longer. My resentment churned inside me, mingling with a bitterness that seemed to have taken root, a relentless ache that no amount of rational thought could quell.

How had it come to this? How had I allowed myself to be bound so completely to a man who only saw me as an extension of his duty? I had hoped—foolishly, perhaps—that Josiah might come to care, that he might offer me something beyond obligation. But instead, all I saw was a reflection of my own despair in his polite, distant gestures. His concern was a performance, his care an act, and I couldn't bear it any longer. I felt like a pawn in a game that had no end, no escape.

I was expected to bring this child into the world, to uphold the honor of the family that Josiah and I had been bound to sustain. The family name, the estate, the line—it all came down to me, to this life I carried without choice, without joy. And yet, every instinct in me rebelled against it, every heartbeat reminded me that I had been trapped in this role, and there was no escape.

A quiet desperation began to stir, a dark whisper that told me I didn't have to carry this burden, that I didn't have to play this part forever. I wanted to be free of it, free of the expectations, the whispers, the carefully constructed life that seemed more like a nightmare with each passing day.

The candlelight flickered across the room, and my gaze settled on the wine decanter, its dark liquid glistening in the glass. I knew it was forbidden, that even a small taste was said to be harmful to the child. And yet, I found myself reaching for it, the weight of my own despair pressing me forward, guiding my hand. I poured a small glass, watching the crimson liquid pool like something forbidden, something defiant.

I took a sip, the wine rich and sharp on my tongue, a hint of bitterness that mirrored my own feelings. The thought crossed my mind—a quiet, desperate thought—that if I could somehow rid myself of this child, if I could free myself from this reminder of my duty, I might finally be able to breathe again. I might finally be free from the ties that bound me to a man who had betrayed me—not through infidelity, but through the coldness that spoke more loudly than any affair ever could.

The wine burned as it went down, a heat that spread through me, but as I took another sip, the warmth quickly turned to discomfort. My stomach churned, a sharp cramp radiating through my abdomen. I winced, setting the glass down as the pain intensified, a low, dull ache that made me clutch at my belly. It hurt, a reminder of the life inside me, a reminder that this child was as real as the anguish that had taken root in my heart.

Tears stung my eyes, blurring the flickering candlelight as I pressed my hand harder against my abdomen, as if trying to force away the pain, the baby, everything that was tying me to this life. But the pressure only made it worse, and I gasped, the pain flaring, a reminder that no amount of desperation would change the reality I faced.

I knew this was not the answer, that no amount of rebellion, no amount of wine, would free me from the life I'd been given. The baby was innocent, a life that had been created not out of love but out of necessity—a necessity that I despised. My heart ached, torn between the helplessness I felt and the fleeting, desperate hope that perhaps there might be a way to escape.

The sharp pangs in my belly subsided, leaving behind a lingering discomfort, a hollow ache that settled deep within me. I looked down at the glass, still half-full, and pushed it away, my fingers trembling. The bitterness of the wine lingered on my tongue, an echo of my own resentment, my own sorrow.

I had wanted to hurt him, to hurt Josiah by rejecting this child—his child. I had wanted to defy him, to take control of my own body, my own fate. But the act had only hurt me, a painful reminder of how powerless I truly was. I felt tears spill over, hot and unchecked, and I allowed myself to cry, the sobs breaking free in the silence of the night.

I thought of Simon—of what could have been, of the love that might have filled our home had things been different. And for the first time, I allowed myself to let go of that dream. Simon was gone, and with him, the future I had imagined. What remained was this—a life with Josiah, a child that neither of us had planned, but one that was growing within me, despite my resentment, despite my sorrow.

As the tears subsided, I felt a strange sense of calm settle over me. It was not acceptance, not yet, but it was something—a quiet resolve to move forward, to face what lay ahead, even if I did so with a heavy heart. I knew that the bitterness would not fade easily, that the resentment might never fully leave me. But I also knew that I could not keep hurting myself, could not keep punishing this innocent life for the choices that had been made for me.

I looked out the window again, at the moonlit garden, the shadows shifting in the soft breeze. I pressed a hand to my aching belly, feeling the faint flutter of movement within. It was real—this child, this life. And though I could not bring myself to feel joy, I knew I had to find a way to survive, to endure.

And maybe, just maybe, there would come a day when I might feel something other than sorrow, something other than pain. But for tonight, I would let the darkness be my companion, and I would hold on to the hope that, one day, I might find a way to be free—from my bitterness, from my grief, and from the memory of a love that could never be.

30

An Unwanted Confession

The moment I stepped back into the house, the head footman approached me, his tone low, his expression troubled. "My Lord, the Duchess... she returned from the gathering rather early, and she appeared... upset."

My heart tightened, and I immediately made my way to her room. Rumors had been circulating since the day we married, and I could only imagine what she might have overheard this time—what cruel stories or twisted tales had been whispered just within earshot. My pulse quickened as I climbed the stairs, my mind racing through the possibilities. Had someone insinuated that she was merely a replacement, a reluctant Duchess bearing the weight of expectations she'd never asked for?

The soft sound of liquid pouring reached me before I even saw her. As I reached her door, I paused, steadying myself before quietly entering. The sight before me stopped me in my tracks: Jemima, slumped in a chair by the window, a half-filled glass of wine clutched in her hand. The dim light cast shadows across her face, accentuating the anguish etched there, her gaze distant, lost.

A pang of fear and frustration struck me. She was pregnant, and I knew well the dangers of alcohol in her condition. But as I looked closer, I saw the despair in her eyes, the quiet resignation. This wasn't rebellion—it was the expression of someone who had long since abandoned hope.

"Jemima," I said quietly, stepping further into the room, my voice betraying a gentleness that belied the tight knot of fear in my chest. "You know wine isn't safe for you now… it's dangerous for the baby."

She didn't look at me, her gaze fixed on the swirling liquid, her fingers brushing the rim of the glass as if I hadn't spoken at all. Her jaw was set, and the silence that stretched between us felt like a gaping chasm. Slowly, she raised the glass, the light from the nearby lamp reflecting off its surface as she brought it to her lips.

"Jemima, please," I pleaded, stepping closer, but her eyes flicked up to meet mine, cold and filled with a raw defiance I hadn't seen before. There was something fierce and broken in that gaze, something that made my breath catch painfully in my chest.

"I don't care, Josiah," she said, her voice low, almost a whisper, yet full of a bitterness that struck me hard.

A chill ran through me. *Why would she say that?*

Those words settled like stones between us, the weight of them making the air feel thick and suffocating. I took a slow breath, trying to keep my voice steady, careful. "Why would you… why would you say that?" I asked, though in my heart, I feared I already knew the answer.

Finally, she looked at me, her eyes hollow, her expression one of barely contained fury. "Because it's *your* baby, Josiah," She paused, her lips trembling as her voice broke, her eyes narrowing as she glared at me. "And I want it to die."

The words fell like a blade, sharp and cold, each syllable cutting through me with a force that left me breathless. I felt my chest tighten, the shock of her hatred sinking in, a visceral blow that left me standing there, frozen.

"Why?" The question escaped my lips, even though I could feel the answer hovering between us.

She exhaled a shaky breath, setting the glass aside with a hand that trembled. "Because," she replied, her voice breaking, "this is *your* child. A constant reminder of everything I never wanted. I didn't choose this. I didn't choose you, this title… or this life."

The honesty in her voice, the sheer depth of her resentment, left me reeling.

My throat tightened, the illusion that perhaps I had begun to reach her shattering before me. Each word she spoke was like a hammer, driving nails into the fragile hope I had clung to. Her anger, her heartbreak, were on full display, and I could see how much she despised everything that bound us together.

"Jemima…" I began, but the words caught in my throat, tangled between understanding and the painful guilt I couldn't deny. I took a careful breath, trying again, forcing my voice to remain soft. "I never wanted you to feel this way. I never wanted this to be a burden for you…"

She looked away, her gaze falling back to the glass in her hand, her fingers trembling slightly. Her lips twisted into a bitter smile, and she let out a quiet, humorless laugh. "You never wanted it?" she echoed, her voice dripping with scorn. "And yet, here we are. I'm carrying your child, and you think you can just make it all better with kind words and empty gestures."

I swallowed hard, the ache in my chest making it difficult to speak. "I won't force you to carry or bear this child if you truly don't want to," I said, my voice barely more than a whisper, each word careful, deliberate. "But please, don't hurt yourself… don't endanger yourself trying to escape."

Her eyes narrowed, her gaze snapping back to mine, and I could see the storm raging within her, the fury and the heartbreak, the hopelessness. "Why should I continue?" she asked, her voice sharp and trembling. "Why should I risk my life for this child? For you?"

The question hung between us, heavy and filled with her desperation. I could see how she was holding herself together, her hands trembling around the glass. I wanted to reach out, to touch her, to comfort her, but I sensed that any movement might cause her to shatter.

I took a careful step closer, speaking slowly, hoping to reach her beyond the wall of anger. "You don't have to do this for me, Jemima. I know I can't understand what you're going through, and I can't make this any easier. But it's too late for this to be anything but dangerous. You're more than sixteen weeks along now, and if…" I hesitated, trying to find the right words. "If the baby dies, it could harm you. Please, don't risk your life trying to escape."

Her face crumpled, her lips trembling as she clutched the glass tighter, her knuckles whitening. She looked at me, her eyes filled with tears, her voice barely above a whisper. "I hate this. I hate everything about this. And I hate you for putting me here."

The words hit me like a blow, the pain of them sinking deep. I watched as her tears spilled over, her sobs breaking through the anger, raw and filled with anguish. She pressed her hand to her face, her body sagging as though my words had drained what little resolve she had left. Her hand fell to her side, and for the first time, I saw her, truly saw her—lost, fragile, and utterly alone. She released the glass, letting it slip from her fingers, and I lunged forward, catching it before it could shatter against the floor.

I set it on the table behind me, then knelt before her as she folded in on herself, her hands covering her face. Without thinking, I reached forward, pulling her into my arms, drawing her close as she broke down completely. Her shoulders shook with each muffled cry, her defenses crumbling, her vulnerability laid bare.

"It's all right, Jemima," I murmured, my arms wrapped around her, steadying her. "You don't have to do this alone. I'm here. I'll help you in any way I can. Whatever you need, whatever it takes... just let me be here for you."

She leaned into me, her face buried against my shoulder, her body warm and trembling as she let her emotions pour out, raw and unfiltered. Her tears soaked through my shirt, her cries echoing through the stillness of the room. I held her, my heart aching with every sob, every tremor that ran through her.

And as I held her, feeling the weight of her pain, her fear, and her resentment, I vowed silently to be there for her—to find some way to make this life we were bound to something she could bear. I had failed her in so many ways, had let her down at every turn, but here, in this moment, I was determined to be the man she needed, even if it was only one small step at a time.

My own heart heavy with the realization of all she had endured in silence. But in that moment, I was no longer the Duke or her husband. I was simply there for Jemima, holding her as she let the weight of her sorrow spill out, my own tears threatening as I whispered promises I hoped I could keep. Promises that, perhaps one day, she might believe.

As her breathing slowed and her exhaustion overcame her, I carefully laid Jemima down, pulling a blanket over her shoulders with the utmost care. She looked so fragile in that moment, her face pale against the pillow, her eyes closed in what seemed like a rare and almost elusive moment of peace. My heart ached with a mixture of guilt, helplessness, and a protectiveness that I found difficult to put into words. I brushed my hand over her brow, my fingers gliding gently across her skin, feeling the soft, steady rhythm of her breathing. Her vulnerability in that moment was palpable, and it made my chest tighten with emotions I could barely contain.

I leaned closer, my gaze settling on her peaceful expression. My hand rested gently on the curve of her stomach, feeling the faint swell beneath my palm—a delicate reminder of the life we had created together. I closed my eyes, my lips barely parting as I whispered a quiet promise to our unborn child, a promise I hoped I would have the strength to keep. "Stay strong, little one," I murmured, my voice barely a breath in the stillness of the room. "Your mother's just tired, that's all. She'll be all right. I promise you, I'll take care of her. I'll take care of both of you."

I lingered there for a moment longer, feeling the warmth of her skin beneath my hand, willing my words to be true, hoping that somehow, even in her sleep, she could feel my commitment, my determination to see her through this. In that dim light, with the weight of her sorrow still heavy in the air, I realized just how much this child's life—her safety, her future—meant to me. And beyond that, how deeply I wanted this family, this fragile connection between us, to hold. It was no longer just about duty or obligation; it was about something far more personal, something that had taken root deep within me, growing with each passing day.

I stepped out into the hallway and summoned the head servant, my voice low but resolute. My mind was still heavy with the image of Jemima, her exhaustion and vulnerability. I knew I needed to act, even if it meant making decisions that might upset her.

"Remove every bottle of wine, every decanter of spirits," I instructed quietly, my tone leaving no room for debate. "There's to be no alcohol in this house until further notice."

The servant looked startled, his eyes widening slightly as he took in my words. He opened his mouth as if to question me, confusion etched across his face, but I shook my head, my expression firm, signaling that I wouldn't hear any protests. I could see the hesitation in his eyes, the uncertainty, but I couldn't afford any hesitation in this.

"No exceptions," I added, my voice softening just a fraction, though the determination remained. "This is for her well-being, and it is not up for discussion."

Even if Jemima sought solace in other ways, even if she resented me for this act, I would do everything in my power to protect her and the child. I knew this decision would seem harsh, perhaps even controlling, but I couldn't risk anything that might harm her or our unborn child. She might not understand now, might even hate me for it, but her safety—their safety—was worth any cost. I hoped, in time, she would see that my actions were born not out of authority, but out of love and concern.

As I watched the servant hurry away to fulfill my orders, I took a deep breath, trying to steady the emotions that swirled within me. I returned to the doorway of Jemima's room, pausing for a moment to look at her one last time before leaving her to rest. She looked so small, so worn, and yet there was a quiet strength in her, a resilience that had kept her going despite everything. I only hoped that my actions, however harsh they might seem, would give her the space and the chance to find that strength again.

"Rest well, Jemima," I whispered, my voice barely audible, a promise carried on the still air. And with that, I turned and left, the door closing softly behind me, my heart heavy but resolute in the path I had chosen.

31

The Unwanted Resilience

The morning dawned with an unusual quiet, the air thick with tension that hung between Josiah and me, though neither of us dared to speak of it. I could hear his voice murmuring softly with the doctor in the hall outside my room, their conversation low and urgent. I pulled the covers around me, a flicker of resentment flaring at the fact that Josiah had called the doctor so quickly, as if I were some child who needed managing, as if my own choices were not mine to make.

But I felt more than resentment. Shame lingered, unbidden and unwelcome, creeping over me as I replayed the previous night in my mind—my anger, my frustration, the way I had lashed out, declaring that I wanted this child to die. Josiah had said nothing, his face a mask of calm, though I had seen the hurt flash in his eyes, the quiet resignation that told me he had taken my words to heart.

The door creaked open, and Josiah entered with the doctor, his gaze wary as he nodded to me. "Jemima," he said gently, "the doctor is here to check on... on you and the baby. He's going to make sure everything is all right."

I looked away, feeling my cheeks heat as I tried to ignore the way my heart clenched at his words. I'd spent so much time wishing to be free of this child, of the life it represented, yet now the thought of anyone truly knowing the extent of my desperation made me feel raw, exposed in a way I hadn't anticipated.

The doctor approached, his expression professional but softened with understanding. He must have sensed the tension; he kept his voice low and steady as he set his instruments on the bedside table. "Your Grace," he began, his gaze shifting between Josiah and me, "I'd like to do a brief examination, just to make sure everything is progressing well."

I nodded stiffly, feeling Josiah's watchful presence beside me as the doctor took my hand and guided me to lie back against the pillows. He pressed gently on my abdomen, feeling for movement, his fingers skilled and careful as he worked. I held my breath, torn between the desire for something to be wrong and the unsettling feeling that I might regret that wish.

After several moments, he withdrew his hands, his gaze settling on mine with a look of quiet relief that immediately set me on edge.

"Well, Your Grace," he said with a slight smile, "the child is strong. There's no indication of distress, and despite... the circumstances, I believe everything is progressing as expected."

A strange mixture of emotions swirled within me at his words—disappointment, resentment, and a tiny, unwelcome thread of relief. But mostly, I felt a hollow ache, as though some part of me had been denied the escape I so desperately sought.

"The child is unharmed, then?" Josiah asked, his voice steady, but I could sense the weight of his concern, the tension in his posture as he waited for the doctor's confirmation.

The doctor nodded, his tone reassuring. "Yes, it seems so. But as a precaution, I would advise that the Duchess avoid any more... unnecessary risks. Alcohol can have unpredictable effects on an unborn child, especially during this early stage. We've been fortunate this time, but I wouldn't risk it again, Your Grace."

Josiah nodded, his shoulders relaxing just slightly, as though he'd been holding his breath. I could feel his relief radiating from him, though he said nothing, simply lowering himself into the chair beside my bed, his gaze never leaving me. I could see the care in his expression, the quiet worry that he tried to mask, though it only deepened the ache within me.

The doctor finished his examination, giving us a few last words of advice before he packed his things and left, leaving us in silence. Josiah stayed beside me, his hand resting on the edge of the bed, his fingers twitching slightly as if he were resisting the urge to reach out.

"Jemima," he murmured after a long moment, his voice careful, as though he were testing the weight of my name. "I... I'm relieved that the child is unharmed. But please, if there's ever anything you need, or if you're feeling... overwhelmed, I hope you'll let me know."

I looked away, the shame and resentment swirling together, a storm that refused to be quelled. "You don't understand, Josiah," I said quietly, my voice tight. "I don't need pity. I don't need sympathy. I need my own life, my own choices. And this child... this child is just a reminder of everything I never wanted."

His face fell, but he held my gaze, unwavering, a quiet resilience in his eyes. "I know this is hard for you," he replied gently, his voice filled with a patience that only heightened my anger. "I can't begin to understand what you're going through, but I want to try. I want to be here for you, whatever that looks like."

I scoffed, my hands clenching around the sheets. "You say that as if you can solve this. As if your concern, your care, can erase the reality of what's happening."

He didn't flinch, didn't look away. "Maybe I can't," he said softly. "But I can be here. I can shoulder some of this, if you'll let me. And, Jemima..." He hesitated, his voice breaking slightly. "I want to believe that, one day, this child might bring you something... something more than pain."

I felt tears prick at my eyes, unbidden and unwanted. I turned away from him, my voice trembling as I spoke. "I don't need you to try to make me feel better, Josiah. I just... I just need to find a way to get through this on my own."

He didn't respond, but I felt the warmth of his presence, the quiet steadiness that seemed unbreakable, no matter how many walls I tried to place between us.

The doctor's words echoed in my mind—*the child is strong.* I could feel the bitterness seeping back in, hardening my heart against the quiet comfort Josiah offered. This child, this unwanted reminder of everything I'd been forced into, was determined to survive, to thrive, even in the face of my own resentment.

But as I lay there, Josiah's hand hovering beside mine, I felt a flicker of something I couldn't name—a small, reluctant warmth that, try as I might, refused to be snuffed out. It wasn't forgiveness, or acceptance, but it was something, a glimmer of hope that maybe, just maybe, I might find a way through this darkness.

And though I didn't know if I could ever embrace this child, or this life, a part of me couldn't deny the possibility that perhaps, one day, I might find a reason to try.

32

An Uneasy Truce

The days following my confession to Josiah felt strange, as though something fragile and unspoken had settled between us, delicate as a spider's web. The rawness of my words—of my own desperation—still weighed on me, a lingering reminder of the pain I had unleashed. Yet Josiah had not responded with anger or even disappointment. Instead, he had simply been there, unmovable and quietly accepting, absorbing my pain without defense.

I expected him to withdraw, to leave me to my isolation. But Josiah, to my surprise, only became more present—though never intrusive, never overbearing. He would linger in the background, managing his duties with a quiet diligence, but I sensed that his gaze was always on me, that every action he took was somehow designed to ease my discomfort.

One morning, I woke to find that a fresh bouquet of wildflowers had been placed on my windowsill, their soft lavender and pale pink blossoms brightening the room. Next to it, a small note: *"For a gentler morning."*

I felt a reluctant warmth stir within me, though I brushed it aside quickly, reminding myself not to read too much into simple gestures. And yet, each day, there was something small, a subtle reminder that he was there, quietly attentive in ways I had not expected. He began arranging for walks in the nearby meadow, always choosing the paths with the softest incline, a consideration I hadn't asked for but noticed nonetheless.

One afternoon, as I took one of those walks, I paused by a bench overlooking a small grove. I sank onto the seat, feeling the familiar weight of my hand over my belly, my thoughts conflicted as I took in the view. I had never asked him to care for me, never asked him to make these gestures. And yet, they had appeared, day after day, quiet and consistent as the sunrise. His actions spoke of a concern that was somehow separate from duty. I had always thought him bound only by the expectations of our titles, but there was something else here—an unspoken care that I couldn't entirely deny.

When I returned to the manor that evening, I found a physician quietly waiting for me in the sitting room, a new tonic at the ready. Josiah must have arranged it, for he met me at the door and explained in his calm, even tone, "I asked the doctor for something to ease the nausea. He believes it may help you sleep better as well."

I studied him, this man who had been little more than a stranger until recently. "Thank you," I murmured, trying not to let him see the hint of warmth his words brought. It was just a tonic, just another practical arrangement, but I felt a reluctant gratitude all the same.

He smiled slightly, his eyes softening. "I only want to make this easier for you, Jemima."

The words lingered in the air, and for the first time, I allowed myself to acknowledge the gentleness in his gaze, the sincerity that seemed so unlike the man I had assumed him to be. Perhaps he was just dutiful, a man fulfilling his obligations. But something told me there was more, something deeper that couldn't simply be attributed to his role.

In the weeks that followed, Josiah's attentions continued, though he never pressed me, never demanded anything. He kept his distance, aware of my own hesitations, and yet his presence was always there, a quiet support that I began to lean on more than I wanted to admit. He would be in his study, managing estate matters with an unwavering focus, yet I felt his watchful care even from afar.

Each day, I found myself looking for those small gestures, those thoughtful reminders that I was not alone in this. I fought the growing sense of comfort he provided, still resentful of the circumstances that had forced us together.

But the walls I'd built around my heart began to show cracks, faint and fragile.

One evening, I passed by his study on my way to bed and heard his voice, low and serious, speaking with Benjamin, his closest friend. I paused by the door, the words drifting through the half-opened door.

"...I only hope she finds some peace," he was saying. "I can see her pain, and I know I'm part of that. I just want her to know she's... she's not alone."

The quiet sincerity of his words struck me, pulling at something I'd kept buried. Josiah's voice, steady and filled with an earnestness I hadn't expected, resonated with a warmth that I hadn't allowed myself to see. He wasn't trying to bind me further, wasn't pushing his expectations onto me. He was simply... here. And as much as I wanted to dismiss it, to push him away, I couldn't help but feel the smallest flicker of respect for him, a begrudging admiration that was all the more powerful for how unexpected it was.

Over time, that flicker grew, a fragile understanding that began to bridge the gap between us. I stopped avoiding him quite so rigorously; instead, I'd catch his eye in passing, perhaps even offer a nod or a quiet greeting. In return, he never pressed, only continued with his steady care, his small gestures that had slowly, reluctantly, begun to soften the bitterness within me.

One afternoon, he found me reading in the garden and, without a word, took the seat beside me. We sat in a comfortable silence, the soft breeze rustling through the leaves as he picked up a book and began to read beside me. There was no demand, no expectation in his presence, only a quiet companionship that I found surprisingly easy to settle into.

As the sun dipped lower, casting a golden glow over the garden, I felt the beginnings of a new feeling take root, faint and delicate, as though my heart had dared to hope for the first time in years. It wasn't love, not yet. But it was something—an acknowledgment that he was, perhaps, more than I'd allowed myself to see.

When he finally closed his book, he turned to me, his expression softened by the evening light. "Jemima," he said quietly, as though weighing his words carefully. "I know this has been difficult for both of us. But I want you to know... I don't take this lightly. I don't take *you* lightly."

I looked away, feeling my cheeks warm under his gaze, the truth of his words settling somewhere deep within me. I had resisted his care, fought against the kindness he'd shown, clinging to the bitterness that had once been my shield. But now, with him beside me, his voice filled with sincerity, I found that shield slipping, leaving me open to something I wasn't sure I understood.

"Thank you, Josiah," I whispered, the words escaping before I could hold them back. "For everything."

He nodded, a small, genuine smile curving his lips, a rare softness in his eyes. And in that moment, I realized that a fragile peace had settled between us—a tentative understanding built not on duty, but on the quiet, steady foundation of trust.

As we sat together, the garden fading into twilight, I felt, for the first time, that perhaps—just perhaps—a new life could be forged from the ashes of our resentment. And though I couldn't say where it might lead, a small part of me dared to hope that it could be something more than either of us had ever expected.

33

The Truth Revealed

The last person I expected to see that morning was my mother.

The butler announced her arrival in his usual calm, measured way, but as I made my way to the parlor, I felt an unease settling over me. She hadn't visited since my marriage to Josiah, sending only the occasional letter, filled with the same subtle admonishments and polite encouragements I'd known since girlhood. Her arrival now, after all this time, could only mean one thing: she had heard about my slip, about the wine, and the rumors.

I entered the room slowly, taking a moment to observe her from the doorway. She was perched on the settee, as regal as ever, her back straight, her gloved hands folded neatly in her lap. Despite the formality of her appearance, there was a familiar warmth in her eyes as they settled on me.

"Jemima," she greeted, her tone both affectionate and laced with subtle reproach. She patted the seat beside her, motioning for me to sit.

I crossed the room and sat beside her, acutely aware of the vulnerability I must have exuded. She took my hand in hers, giving it a gentle squeeze, as if to remind me that, for all her severity, she was still my mother.

"Tell me, my dear," she began softly, though I could sense the underlying steel in her voice. "Is it true? You've been drinking?"

Heat rose to my cheeks, and I looked down, ashamed but unwilling to deny it. "It was one glass, Mother. And... I wasn't thinking clearly. There were things said about Josiah—about the legitimacy of this child, about his... supposed indiscretions." My voice wavered as I relived the humiliation, the anger that had pushed me to that point. "I just... I couldn't bear it."

Her lips thinned, and I saw a flicker of understanding in her eyes, though she kept her tone firm. "You cannot allow yourself to be led by gossip, Jemima. You are a Duchess now, and your actions reflect more than just your own feelings. I know the pressure must feel unbearable at times, but that child is an innocent, regardless of the circumstances that brought him here."

I nodded, unable to look her in the eye, but she held my gaze firmly, her expression softening as she continued.

"These rumors, Jemima," she said gently, "have you not questioned where they came from?"

I felt a flash of irritation. "It doesn't matter where they came from," I replied, bitterness slipping into my voice. "Everyone seems to believe them, and for all I know, there's some truth to it. Josiah and his... reputation..."

Mother shook her head, her eyes narrowing slightly. "You've been misled, Jemima. Those rumors—those tales of debauchery and indiscretions—they have nothing to do with your husband. They were Simon's."

I looked up sharply, taken aback by her words. "Simon's?"

"Yes." She spoke with a certainty that left no room for doubt. "Your late fiancé was... not the man you believed him to be. Much of the family knew of his habits, of his... indiscretions, and yet he was protected, his reputation kept intact. And Josiah, well, he bore the brunt of those whispers to keep his brother's name—and the family name—clean."

The room seemed to shift around me, my vision narrowing as her words sank in. "Josiah took the blame?" I asked, incredulous, my voice barely a whisper.

"Yes, Jemima." She nodded, her eyes steady. "Josiah may be reserved, and perhaps he lacks the charm that Simon exuded, but he is a man of character, a man who has made sacrifices to preserve the family's honor. He endured those rumors, those whispers, so that Simon could remain the golden child in society's eyes."

A weight settled in my chest, an uncomfortable, tangled mix of relief and guilt. I thought of all the times I'd judged him, resented him for faults that had never been his. The rumors, the supposed indiscretions, the whispers that had haunted my own life—all of it had been Simon's doing, Simon's legacy. And Josiah had borne the weight of it quietly, without retaliation, without complaint.

My mother watched me closely, sensing my inner turmoil. "Jemima," she said, her tone softer now, almost gentle. "You married the right man. Not a perfect one, no, but one who has shown more grace, more honor than many men in his position might have."

I let out a shaky breath, my mind racing. It felt as though a veil had been lifted, revealing a truth I had been unwilling to see. Josiah was not the cold, indifferent man I had believed him to be. He was far from the villain I had painted in my mind. Instead, he was someone who had quietly shouldered burdens, who had shown kindness even in the face of my resentment, who had treated me with care even when I had been determined to shut him out.

My mother continued, her voice calm but firm. "You must see that he cares for you, Jemima. Perhaps more deeply than you realize. It would do you well to let go of the bitterness, to recognize that not all men are like Simon. Josiah has shown himself to be a man worthy of respect, and perhaps even affection."

Affection. The word felt foreign, almost strange when applied to my marriage. And yet, in that moment, I realized I could not deny it. My heart had softened toward Josiah, bit by bit, in ways I had not fully acknowledged until now. I thought of the gentle notes he had left, the walks he had arranged, the way he had held me without judgment on the night I had broken down.

"He never said a word," I whispered, more to myself than to her, feeling the sharp ache of guilt twist within me. "He could have defended himself, but he never did. He just... he let me believe..."

Mother nodded, her expression patient. "Because he cares, Jemima. He would rather you hate him than disparage the memory of his brother, flawed as Simon may have been."

I swallowed, my throat tight as I absorbed the weight of her words. There was no denying the truth now, no escaping the reality that I had misjudged Josiah, that I had allowed my own fears and insecurities to cloud my perception of him. He was not the man I had imagined him to be. He was better.

Slowly, I looked up at her, feeling a new resolve settle within me. "I didn't realize… I never allowed myself to see him as he truly is. I was so wrapped up in my own resentment, my own fear."

She squeezed my hand gently, a rare gesture of affection that I hadn't felt in years. "Then see him now, Jemima. Let go of the past, and open your heart to the possibility that perhaps this marriage—though far from perfect—can become something more than duty."

I nodded, a strange sense of calm washing over me as her words settled. I had been given a new truth, a new lens through which to view Josiah. My mother explained that she had only recently learned the full extent of Simon's indiscretions from other family members who, out of misplaced loyalty, had kept her in the dark for years. She regretted not telling me sooner, but she hadn't known herself until after my marriage. The realization that even my mother had been deceived made the truth hit harder, yet it also offered a sense of closure. And as I sat there, my heart heavy with both regret and a budding hope, I found myself willing, perhaps for the first time, to see my husband for who he truly was.

As Mother left, I sat in the quiet parlor, staring at the place where she had been, her words lingering in my mind. I knew that the path forward would not be simple, that I had a lifetime of resentment to unravel. But for the first time, I felt a glimmer of something other than anger, something that felt almost like relief.

Perhaps, despite the cold and bitter beginnings, there was a chance—a small, fragile chance—that a new life, a new bond, could be forged between us. And perhaps, just perhaps, I could find it in my heart to truly open myself to the man I had married, to the man who had shown me kindness and patience despite everything.

And with that thought, I rose, feeling a quiet strength within me, ready to face whatever lay ahead.

34

The Apology

The house was quiet as I moved through the corridors, the low afternoon light casting soft shadows against the walls. My mother's words lingered, echoing in my mind like a quiet chant, each one chipping away at the walls I had built so carefully around myself. I had been wrong. So deeply, painfully wrong about Josiah. I had painted him with the same brush I had used for Simon, seeing him as a man burdened by duty, a stranger I could never truly trust. But in truth, he had been the one bearing Simon's sins in silence, quietly enduring the whispers, the suspicion, the weight of my resentment—all to honor the memory of a brother who hadn't deserved it.

Guilt twisted within me, an ache that sharpened with each step I took toward the drawing room. How many times had I misjudged him? How many times had I turned away from his small gestures of care, viewing them as mere duty when, all along, he had been reaching out to me? My heart tightened at the realization, and I knew I had to make this right—somehow.

The door was open just enough for me to see him, seated at his desk, poring over estate ledgers and documents with his usual diligence. The sight of him, so focused, so quietly intent, made my heart clench. He had carried so much, so steadily, without complaint, while I had only added to his burden.

I took a steadying breath and stepped inside, closing the door softly behind me. He looked up, his eyes registering surprise as he saw me standing there.

But he quickly masked it, setting down his pen and rising to his feet, his expression polite and restrained.

"Jemima," he said quietly, inclining his head. "Is there something you need?"

For a moment, I was silent, simply looking at him, allowing myself to truly see him as he was—the man who had been kind to me when I had deserved only silence, who had shown patience where others might have shown frustration. The man who, despite everything, had never given up on trying to reach me.

"I... I came to apologize," I said softly, my voice trembling despite my resolve.

Josiah's brow furrowed, his expression shifting from surprise to confusion. "Apologize? Jemima, I... I don't understand. Why now? What brought this on?"

"I Apologized for everything, Josiah. For misjudging you, for seeing you through the wrong lens. I believed things about you that... that were never true. And I've come to realize how unfair I've been."

He watched me carefully, his expression softening as my words settled between us. I saw the flicker of emotion in his eyes—something like relief mingled with hesitation—as though he were afraid to believe that my apology was genuine. He opened his mouth to speak, but no words came at first, and he seemed to struggle to find the right response.

"Jemima," he began, his voice barely a whisper, filled with confusion. "You don't need to apologize. You've been through so much—"

"No," I interrupted, shaking my head, my eyes misting. "I do. I need to apologize, because you've been nothing but kind to me, and I've only responded with anger and resentment. You've been carrying burdens that weren't yours, and I never stopped to see that." My voice cracked, and I took a shaky breath, trying to steady myself.

He was quiet, his gaze fixed on mine, his eyes searching, as though he were trying to understand this shift, this newfound softness in my tone. And for the first time, I didn't resist the warmth that rose in me, the quiet, trembling hope that perhaps this could be the beginning of something new.

I took a step closer, then another, until I was standing just in front of him.

My heart raced, my pulse a drumbeat of nerves and longing, and yet I felt a quiet strength within me—a certainty I hadn't felt in a long time.

"Josiah," I whispered, my voice wavering as I lifted a hand to his cheek. He stiffened slightly, his eyes widening at the unexpected touch, and I could see the confusion still lingering there, as if he wasn't quite sure if this was real. "I see you now. I see the man you are, and I can't believe it took me so long to understand."

Before I could think, before I could second-guess myself, I leaned in, pressing my lips softly to his—a kiss that was equal parts apology and hope, a gesture that held everything I hadn't been able to say. I felt him freeze for a moment, as if caught off guard, but then his hand moved to my waist, drawing me closer, his other hand cradling my cheek as he returned the kiss, gentle and steady, filled with the quiet tenderness he had shown me in every action, every glance.

When we finally pulled apart, his eyes searched mine, his expression open and vulnerable in a way I had never seen before. "Jemima," he murmured, his voice low and rough with emotion, "what brought this on? I... I don't understand."

I let out a shaky breath, my fingers brushing his cheek, my heart aching with the weight of everything I needed to say. "My mother made me realize... I was wrong about you. I thought you were just another version of Simon—someone who only cared about the title, about duty. But you're not. You've been here, carrying everything without complaint, trying to make this place a home for me. I see that now, and I'm so sorry it took me so long."

His gaze softened, and I saw the hint of a smile, small but genuine, tugging at his lips. "You don't have to apologize, Jemima. I never expected anything from you... I only wanted to give you what I could."

I felt my chest tighten, a warmth spreading through me as I looked up at him, the hope in his eyes mirrored in my own. "You've given me more than I ever thought I could have," I whispered, my voice breaking. "You've given me patience, kindness—you've given me a chance to see that maybe this life isn't a prison after all."

His hand moved to rest on my growing belly, a subtle but unmistakable gesture of care, of acknowledgment for the life we were bringing into the world together. I placed my hand over his, my fingers curling around his, and in that touch, I felt a promise—an unspoken vow that he would stand by me, that we would face whatever lay ahead, not as two strangers bound by duty, but as partners, perhaps even as something more.

"Thank you for seeing me," he said, his voice barely more than a whisper, filled with a raw honesty that made my heart swell. I nodded, tears welling in my eyes, and as he pulled me into his arms, holding me close, I knew that we had taken our first true step forward—one built on trust, on understanding, and perhaps, one day, on love.

He stayed close, his forehead resting gently against mine, his breath steady, grounding. "And I'm sorry, Jemima," he whispered. "I thought I was protecting you, sparing you from the truth. But all I did was create distance, give you reason to doubt me. And that's... that's my regret."

I could feel his regret, the sorrow lacing his words as he held me close, his fingers gentle against my skin, his touch filled with a tenderness that made my heart ache. I'd spent so long resenting him, viewing him as the shadow of Simon, yet here he was, steady and present, offering me the care and honesty I hadn't known I needed.

"I want you to know, Jemima," he continued, his voice a quiet promise, "that I'll be the husband you deserve—from this moment on. No secrets, no half-truths. Just... me. All of me."

35

Unspoken Regrets and New Promises

I could hardly breathe, caught in the depth of her gaze, the warmth of her touch as she stood before me. Jemima's apology, her quiet admission of seeing me in a new light, felt like a balm on a wound I hadn't realized was still raw. Her fingers rested gently on my cheek, her eyes bright and sincere, as though she were seeing me for the first time. And as she leaned forward, her lips brushing mine, I felt a shudder of emotion wash over me, a sense of relief mingled with a fragile hope I scarcely dared to hold.

When we broke apart, she looked up at me, her face open, vulnerable, words heavy with meaning that went far beyond a simple apology. It was an acknowledgment, a tentative acceptance of who I truly was, rather than the shadow of Simon or the weight of duty. I searched her eyes, caught off guard by the tenderness there, and in that moment, I knew I could no longer hide my truth from her. She deserved to know everything.

"Jemima," I murmured, my voice barely steady, "there's something you must understand. I've tried to protect you, or at least I thought I was. But in reality, I was shielding you from things you had every right to know, and it cost us both."

She looked at me with soft curiosity, her hand still on my cheek, as though willing me to go on.

"It was Simon," I continued, my voice low, steadying myself as I confessed, "who was behind the rumors, the indiscretions, the scandals. Not me. And

I... I let everyone believe otherwise because I thought it was my duty to protect his memory, to keep the family reputation intact. But all it did was give you reason to resent me, and I regret that more than I can say."

She was silent, her expression attentive and thoughtful. There was a pause, and I could feel the weight of what I was about to say settling between us, a piece of the truth that I knew had fueled her distrust more than anything else.

"I imagine you've heard the rumors of an illegitimate child," I went on, and her eyes flickered with a hint of uncertainty. "It's true, Jemima. There is a child—but it wasn't mine. It was Simon's. He had a... liaison, hidden from the family, with a young woman who bore his child."

Her breath hitched softly, and I pressed on, feeling the need to explain fully. "After Simon died, I made arrangements for the child's care. I couldn't abandon him to fend for himself, and I felt it was my duty to ensure he would never want for anything. But I did all of this quietly, fearing that revealing the truth would bring shame to our family—and to you."

A silence fell between us as my words settled, but I could see the pieces falling into place in her eyes—the realization that she had held me responsible for a past that wasn't mine.

Her expression softened, and she reached for my hand, her fingers curling around mine. "Josiah," she whispered, her voice filled with an understanding that took me by surprise. "I see that now... and I'm sorry too. I held onto my anger, my resentment, because it was easier than facing the fear, the feeling that I would never be enough in this role, that I would never be enough for you."

I tightened my grip on her hand, feeling an ache at her words, an ache that softened as I saw the vulnerability in her gaze. "Jemima," I murmured, "you've always been more than enough. I only wish I had shown you that sooner."

Her lips trembled, a faint smile breaking through as she let out a shaky breath. "I've been so afraid, Josiah... afraid that I could never measure up, that this life would always feel like a prison. But you've shown me, with your kindness, your patience... you've shown me that maybe it doesn't have to be."

My chest tightened, an overwhelming sense of relief flooding through me as I realized that she was truly letting go—of the anger, of the bitterness, and of the past that had kept us apart. She looked at me, her expression softened by a gentleness that made my heart ache, and I could see that she was finally allowing herself to believe, to hope, to see the possibility of a life beyond the shadows of resentment.

"Jemima," I said, my voice barely above a whisper, "I promise you that I will be the husband you deserve. No more secrets, no more half-truths. I want to give you all of me—every part, nothing hidden."

Her hand moved to rest on her growing belly, a subtle but unmistakable gesture that reminded me of the life we were bringing into the world together, a bond that went beyond duty or expectation. I placed my hand over hers, feeling the warmth of her fingers beneath mine, and in that touch, I felt an unspoken promise, a commitment that was stronger than anything words could convey.

"Thank you," she whispered, her voice filled with a warmth that reached deep within me, melting the final remnants of doubt. "For seeing me, for understanding... and for being willing to start again."

We stood there in the quiet, the late afternoon light casting a soft glow around us, and I knew that this was the beginning of something new—a foundation built on respect, trust, and, perhaps one day, on love. I leaned forward, pressing my forehead gently to hers, our breaths mingling, our hearts aligned in a silent vow that we would face the future together, unburdened by the past.

"I promise," I whispered, the words a quiet reverence, a prayer for the life we were building. "We'll face it all, together."

36

A Father's Promise

I could feel the warmth of Josiah's hands as they moved gently over my swollen legs, his fingers pressing just enough to relieve the aches that had been plaguing me throughout the day. It was strange, this intimacy between us, both comforting and disconcerting. I hadn't expected to find myself here, in his capable hands, his touch filled with care that went beyond simple duty.

As I watched him, my mind drifted back to those early months—how foolish I'd been, so desperate to escape the confines of this life that I'd nearly done something irreversibly cruel. The memory of trying to rid myself of his child, the bitterness that had clouded my heart, filled me with a deep sense of shame. I glanced down at my belly, now round and full, a constant reminder of my past resentment and my current joy. How much had changed since then, how far we'd come.

I shifted slightly, my belly making it difficult to move as freely as I once had. Josiah noticed, pausing in his work to look up at me, his brow creased with concern. "Are you comfortable?" he asked, his voice soft.

I nodded, smiling down at him. "Yes, thank you," I murmured, feeling a warmth rise in my cheeks. "It's just… strange, thinking back on how things were." I let out a soft, embarrassed laugh, my hand resting on my belly. "I feel silly for the things I did, the thoughts I had. And now here I am, more than six months along, with you beside me."

He looked up at me, his expression tender, his hands still resting on my legs. "You had every right to feel how you did, Jemima," he said quietly, his thumb tracing gentle circles on my ankle. "I know I didn't make things easy in the beginning either."

I smiled, placing my hand over his. "Perhaps," I said softly, "but it's different now. I can't imagine going through this without you." My hand moved to my belly, feeling the steady weight of our children within me. "The doctor's diagnosis—when they told us it was twins—I think it was the first time I realized just how much I wanted this... how much I wanted them."

He nodded, his eyes softening as he remembered that day. "I admit, I was surprised too," he said, his voice holding a hint of laughter. "I was worried, seeing how quickly your belly grew. But twins... well, I suppose they're a miracle in themselves."

I could see the flicker of worry in his eyes, a shadow that had been there since the doctor's diagnosis. He hadn't said much, but I knew the fear that lingered within him—the concern for what was to come, for the challenges and risks that accompanied bringing twins into the world.

"Are you scared?" I asked, my voice barely above a whisper. "About... what lies ahead?"

He looked at me, his gaze soft yet serious, his hands gentle as they continued to rub my legs. "A little," he admitted, his voice steady. "I've seen how difficult labor can be, and with twins, there's always a risk. I just... I worry for you, Jemima. I want you and the babies to be safe."

His honesty touched me deeply, and without thinking, I leaned forward, wrapping my arms around him. His arms came around me without hesitation, his hands pressing gently against my back as he held me close. "It's all right, Josiah," I murmured against his shoulder. "We'll face it together. I know it will be difficult, but I'm not afraid anymore."

He pulled back slightly, his gaze meeting mine, filled with a mixture of tenderness and gratitude that made my heart ache. Carefully, he shifted me onto his lap, his hands supporting my weight as he adjusted, making sure I was comfortable. He was always so thoughtful, so quietly protective, and it made me feel safe in a way I hadn't felt in a long time.

His hand moved to rest on my belly, his fingers splayed over the rounded curve. He rubbed gently, his touch filled with reverence, and I felt a shiver of warmth spread through me. There was something incredibly soothing in the way he touched me, as though his hands could somehow ease the discomfort, the tension, even the lingering fears.

I looked up at him, hesitating before I spoke, my voice softer than I'd intended. "Will you... will you be there when the time comes? When I go into labor?"

He looked at me with surprise, then nodded, his hand still resting on my belly. "Of course," he said quietly, his voice filled with conviction. "Where else would I be, if not by your side?"

His words wrapped around me like a promise, a vow that I knew he would keep no matter what. He was steady, unwavering, the kind of man who would never abandon me, no matter the trials we might face. And in that moment, I felt a peace settle over me, a quiet assurance that whatever lay ahead, we would face it together.

He leaned down, his hand still on my belly, his voice a low, soothing murmur. "You two," he whispered, as though speaking directly to our children, "listen to your mother, now. Come into this world easily, without trouble, so she won't have to struggle. Do you hear me?"

And just as he finished speaking, I felt a sharp, unexpected kick, as though one of the babies was responding to his words. I gasped, a smile breaking across my face, and I looked up at him, seeing the delight mirrored in his eyes.

"Did you feel that?" I whispered, my voice filled with wonder.

He nodded, his expression a mixture of surprise and joy as he continued to rub my belly, his hand lingering over the spot where the kick had been. "They're listening," he said softly, a smile tugging at his lips. "Perhaps they know who's speaking to them."

We stayed like that, his hand on my belly, his other arm wrapped securely around me, and for the first time, I allowed myself to fully embrace the love and joy that had grown between us. The memory of my earlier resentment, my doubts, faded into nothingness, replaced by a profound sense of gratitude, a quiet, steady love that I knew would only deepen with time.

In that quiet moment, with his hand on our children and his promise filling the air between us, I felt a warmth unlike any I had ever known. It was a warmth that came not from duty or obligation, but from a love that had blossomed slowly, steadily, a love that would carry us through whatever lay ahead.

And as I leaned into him, feeling the gentle rhythm of his breath, I knew that this—this life, this family—was all I had ever wanted.

37

The Journey Home

As the carriage rolled to a stop before my family's estate, I felt a flutter in my chest, a mix of excitement and nerves. It had been months since I'd last seen my family, and in that time, so much had changed—not only my life with Josiah but within me as well. I was different now, and I hoped that they would see that, that they would understand.

The door of the carriage swung open, and Josiah offered his hand, his eyes softening as he looked at me. "Take your time," he said gently, as I carefully shifted my weight. My movements had grown slower, heavier—the sizable curve of my belly now undeniable. I took his hand gratefully, feeling the warmth of his touch steadying me as I stepped down from the carriage.

Standing on the familiar gravel path, I took in the sight of the estate, my heart swelling with nostalgia. Before I could fully gather myself, I heard my mother's voice ringing out, full of warmth and joy.

"Jemima! Josiah!" My mother descended the steps with my father right behind her, both of them beaming with pride. The sight of them made my heart swell—the warmth of their smiles, the open joy in their eyes.

"Mother," I breathed, wrapping my arms around her as best I could, my belly making the gesture somewhat awkward but no less heartfelt. My father stepped forward as well, enveloping me in a gentle hug, his hand resting protectively on my back.

"My darling girl," he murmured, his voice filled with emotion. "Look at you—absolutely glowing."

They both stepped back to take me in, their eyes settling on my swollen belly with a mixture of awe and wonder. My mother placed a hand over her mouth, her eyes misting as she took in the sight.

"Twins," she whispered, her voice trembling. "Oh, Jemima, it's extraordinary! And look at you—positively radiant."

I felt my cheeks warm at her praise, nodding slightly as my hand moved instinctively to rest on my belly. "Yes, twins. It was quite a surprise, wasn't it, Josiah?" I glanced over at him, a small smile tugging at my lips.

Josiah chuckled softly, slipping his arm around my waist in a gesture that felt natural now—comforting. "To say the least," he said, a playful glint in his eyes. "I'll admit, I was rather worried when I first noticed how quickly she was growing." He paused, giving me an affectionate look. "I thought perhaps something was amiss, but the doctor assured us that all was well—just more than we'd bargained for."

Laughter rippled through the group, warmth and comfort filling the air. Josiah's hand rested gently on my back, his thumb tracing small, soothing circles. It was a simple gesture, but it steadied me, grounding me in the joy of this moment.

"Oh, Jemima!" a familiar voice called, and I looked up just in time to see my sister, Agnes, bounding down the steps, her face alight with excitement. She threw her arms around me in a careful hug, her eyes shining as she stepped back, her hands resting lightly on my shoulders. "You look beautiful! I can't believe it—twins! You're absolutely radiant."

I smiled at her, my heart swelling with affection. "Thank you, Agnes. But enough about me—Mother tells me congratulations are in order for you as well."

Her grin widened, her cheeks flushing with happiness. "Yes! Can you believe it? I'm engaged!" She turned to Josiah, giving him a curtsy. "Thank you for bringing her home, Your Grace. It means the world to have my sister here."

Josiah inclined his head, his smile gentle. "The honor is ours, Agnes. I wouldn't dream of letting Jemima miss such an important moment."

Agnes's joy was infectious, and as she led us inside, I felt a renewed sense of peace settle within me. My family, once strained by tension and unspoken expectations, now welcomed us with open arms, embracing Josiah and me with a warmth that felt like home.

We were soon seated in the drawing room, surrounded by laughter and conversation. My mother fussed over every comfort I might need—adjusting cushions, insisting on a cup of tea—all delivered with an attentive fondness that reminded me of how much I'd missed this.

As the evening wore on, my mother settled beside me, her eyes soft as she placed a gentle hand on my belly. "You must be so proud, Jemima," she murmured, her voice filled with awe. "Two lives growing within you... it's a beautiful thing."

I nodded, a surprising warmth filling my heart. "Yes, Mother. It hasn't been easy, but... I think I'm beginning to understand the beauty in it."

She smiled, her gaze drifting to Josiah, who was deep in conversation with my father across the room. "And Josiah? How is he with all of this? He seems... changed, softened."

I followed her gaze, my heart tightening with a mix of gratitude and affection. "He's been more than I ever expected, Mother. I misjudged him in the beginning, but he's shown me a kindness and patience I didn't think possible. Especially since we found out about the twins... he's been so gentle, so attentive. I don't know what I would have done without him."

She squeezed my hand, her eyes filled with understanding. "Then you chose well, Jemima. You may have had your doubts, but Josiah is a good man—a man who clearly cares for you."

I nodded, a quiet strength settling within me. "Yes. I know that now."

As the evening drew to a close, Josiah came over, his eyes warm as he offered me his hand. "Are you ready to retire, Jemima?" he asked softly, his touch steadying me as I rose from my seat.

"Yes, I think I am," I replied, warmth flooding through me as he guided me toward the stairs. My mother and father bid us goodnight, their smiles tender as they watched us go.

When we reached my old room, Josiah stayed by my side as I settled in, adjusting the covers over my belly with a tenderness that made my heart ache. He looked down at me, his gaze filled with quiet pride and something deeper—something that spoke of the bond we had forged over these months.

"Goodnight, Jemima," he whispered, his hand lingering on mine, his eyes searching mine as if wanting to say more but choosing to hold back.

I looked up at him, feeling the depth of his care in that simple gesture. "Goodnight, Josiah," I murmured, my voice soft with gratitude. As he turned to leave, I reached out, catching his hand. "Thank you… for everything. For bringing me home, for being here."

He paused, his eyes meeting mine, and I saw the faintest hint of emotion there—something unspoken but deeply felt. He squeezed my hand gently, his voice low. "Always, Jemima. I'll always be here."

With that, he left, and I watched the door close softly behind him, a peace settling over me that I hadn't felt in a long time. As I lay back against the pillows, surrounded by the familiarity of my old room, I knew that whatever lay ahead, I was no longer alone. I had my family, I had Josiah, and I had a future that, for the first time in so long, felt filled with hope.

38

A Storm Brewing

The sky darkened ominously as we left my family's estate, thick clouds gathering in rolling waves that seemed to press down on the world below. The air was heavy, oppressive, as if holding its breath in anticipation of the storm. I shifted in my seat, trying to adjust the weight of my belly as it pulled at my body. There was a tightness across my abdomen that came and went in waves, a dull ache that I had told myself was nothing more than the usual discomfort I'd grown accustomed to these past few weeks.

But now, as we bumped along the uneven road, the sensation sharpened, each contraction a little stronger, a little more insistent. I winced and took a slow breath, trying to stay calm. It was probably just false labor, nothing to be concerned about.

Beside me, Josiah sat tense, his eyes scanning the horizon as the first rumbles of thunder echoed in the distance. The unease that had been growing within me seemed to resonate with the storm building outside, and I couldn't shake the creeping sense of dread that clung to me, prickling at my nerves.

Josiah glanced my way, his eyes narrowing with concern as he noticed my discomfort. He took my hand in his, squeezing gently. "Are you all right, Jemima?" he asked, his voice soft, though I could hear the worry in his tone.

I nodded, swallowing hard as I tried to smile. "I'm fine. Just... a bit uncomfortable, that's all. The ride is rougher than I expected."

He nodded, his gaze lingering on me for a moment longer before he looked back out at the horizon. The storm was approaching fast, thick sheets of rain already visible in the distance. I could see the tension in his shoulders, the way his jaw clenched as the thunder grew louder. He kept his hand on mine, a steady reassurance that did little to quell the growing unease within me.

The carriage jolted over a particularly rough patch, and I felt another tightening in my belly—this one sharp enough to steal my breath for a moment. I inhaled slowly, trying to steady myself. It was nothing, just the discomfort of the journey, I told myself again. It would pass.

But as we continued, the pain didn't pass. It grew, the tightening coming in waves, each one stronger than the last. I shifted again, pressing a hand to my abdomen, my breath catching as another wave hit. Josiah's eyes flicked toward me, his brows drawing together in concern.

"Jemima?" he asked again, his voice more urgent this time.

I forced a smile, trying to ignore the gnawing worry in my chest. "It's fine, Josiah. Just a bit of a cramp, I think."

He didn't look convinced, but he nodded, his thumb brushing over my knuckles as he turned his attention back to the road. The sky was growing darker, the wind picking up as the storm closed in around us. The first drops of rain began to fall, quickly turning into a downpour that pounded against the carriage, the sound a relentless drumbeat that filled the air.

I closed my eyes, trying to focus on my breathing, on the rhythmic motion of the carriage. But the road grew rougher, the jolts more jarring, each one sending a fresh wave of pain through my abdomen. The tightness was no longer something I could ignore—it was becoming sharp, insistent, each contraction pulling at me, demanding my attention.

And then, without warning, the carriage lurched to a sudden halt, pitching us forward. I gasped, clutching at Josiah's arm as he wrapped it around me, holding me steady. The horses whinnied in panic, their hooves slipping in the mud as the driver shouted for them to calm.

Josiah leaned forward, his voice tense as he called out to the driver. "Why have we stopped?"

The driver's voice came back, muffled by the rain. "The wheels, Your

Grace—they're stuck! The mud's too thick; I'm afraid we won't be able to move until the storm passes."

I felt a tremor of fear shoot through me as I glanced out the window. The road had turned into a river of mud, the storm raging around us with no sign of stopping. We were trapped, alone, with no shelter and no help.

Another pain tore through my abdomen, sharper this time, and I gasped, my hand flying to my belly. I doubled over slightly, my heart pounding as realization struck—this was no ordinary discomfort. The contractions were real, and they were growing stronger.

"Josiah..." I whispered, my voice trembling as I looked up at him, my eyes wide with panic. "Something's wrong. I think—it's starting."

His face paled, his eyes widening as he processed my words. "Are you sure?" he asked, his voice barely audible over the roar of the rain.

Another contraction hit, fierce and unyielding, leaving no room for doubt. I nodded, clutching at his arm, my voice breaking. "Yes. I'm sure."

He stared at me, his face a mask of shock and fear. His gaze darted toward the window, the storm raging outside, the road turned to a river of mud. The horror in his eyes mirrored my own. We were trapped, with nowhere to go, no help, and the realization left me breathless.

"Jemima," he said, his voice shaking but filled with determination, "I'm here. I won't leave you. No matter what happens, I'm right here."

I nodded, tears stinging my eyes as I tried to steady my breathing, tried to focus on his voice, on the warmth of his hand around mine. But the pain was relentless, each contraction more powerful, more demanding, my body betraying me as it began the process of labor.

The hours stretched on, the storm growing worse as the night deepened. Each contraction was like a wave, crashing over me, leaving me gasping, my body trembling with exhaustion. I could feel the tightness in my belly growing stronger, the pressure building, my entire body straining under the effort. The hint of labor that had begun as a mere discomfort had now taken over, each pain a reminder that I was not in control.

Josiah held me, his voice a constant presence, urging me to breathe, to focus on his words. His arm was around me, his touch steady, his other hand brushing damp strands of hair away from my face. He was my anchor, the one thing that kept me from giving in to the fear that gripped me.

"Listen to me, Jemima," he murmured, his voice gentle but insistent, his hand cupping my cheek. "Breathe with me. We'll get through this. Just focus on me, all right?"

I nodded, clinging to his words, to the warmth of his hand on my face, the steadiness of his presence. He spoke to me softly, his words grounding me as I fought to keep control, to push back the fear that threatened to swallow me whole.

The storm roared outside, the thunder echoing through the carriage, and I could feel my strength waning, each contraction taking more from me, leaving me drained. I didn't know how much longer I could endure, the pain relentless, unyielding. I leaned into Josiah, my face buried against his chest, my hands clutching at his coat, desperate for some sense of comfort, of security.

Suddenly, through the haze of pain, I heard Josiah's voice, fierce with urgency as he called to the driver. "Go find help. Now. The nearest village—there must be someone, a midwife, anyone who can assist us."

The driver hesitated, his voice filled with uncertainty. "Your Grace, the storm—"

"Go!" Josiah's tone left no room for argument, and within moments, the driver was gone, leaving us alone in the carriage as the rain poured down around us.

I looked up at him, tears spilling down my cheeks as another wave of pain tore through me. "Please, Josiah... don't leave me."

He brushed a kiss against my forehead, his touch as gentle as it was resolute. "I won't, Jemima. I swear to you, I'm right here. I won't leave you, not for a moment."

His words were my lifeline, the only thing that kept me from breaking, from surrendering to the terror that gripped me. I held onto him, his presence my anchor, his voice the one steady thing in the chaos of the storm.

Hours passed, each one feeling like a lifetime, the pain unrelenting, my body exhausted. But Josiah was there, his arms around me, his voice soothing, his touch a reminder that I wasn't alone. And as I felt the pain peak, as I faced the storm within and without, I found a strength I hadn't known I possessed—a strength that came from him, from the love I hadn't realized had taken root within me.

    We were alone, surrounded by darkness and thunder, but in that moment, I knew that we would face whatever lay ahead together. And somehow, despite the fear, despite the pain, I began to believe that maybe, just maybe, we would survive this storm. Together.

39

Facing the Ordeal Together

The storm raged on outside, rain hammering against the roof of the carriage in a relentless, rhythmic drumbeat. I clutched Josiah's hand, my knuckles white as another wave of pain tore through me. Each contraction felt sharper, stronger, more unforgiving than the last, and the cramped space of the carriage offered no comfort. The jolting movements over the muddy, uneven road made everything worse—every lurch sent a fresh ripple of pain through my spine and belly. I could hardly move, trapped in this small, swaying box, the walls pressing in around me as the contractions gripped me unrelentingly.

Josiah was beside me, his hands steady and sure, his voice a constant, soothing murmur as he brushed the damp hair from my face. His touch was gentle, a lifeline as I struggled through each wave. "Breathe, Jemima," he whispered, his hand finding mine, squeezing in a way that seemed to ground me. "Just focus on breathing. I'm here, right here with you."

I tried, gasping for air, my chest tightening with each sharp breath as the pain threatened to overwhelm me. Tears blurred my vision, and I looked at him, my voice trembling as I whispered, "Josiah, I don't... I don't think I can..." My voice cracked, the words escaping me in a desperate plea.

He looked at me, his eyes full of fierce determination, filled with a tenderness that took my breath away. "Yes, you can," he said, his voice unwavering. "You're stronger than you know, Jemima. Just hold on to me."

Another contraction gripped me, a fierce wave that radiated down to my bones, leaving me shaking. I squeezed his hand tightly, the intensity of the pain stealing my breath. The ache was all-consuming, pulling me under, and I cried out, my breaths coming in shallow, frantic gasps. My body trembled, unable to fight against the relentless agony.

"Oh, Josiah, why does it hurt so much? Why—" I gasped, my entire body shuddering with the force of each contraction.

He held me closer, his arm wrapping around my shoulders as his free hand rested at the curve of my belly, warm and reassuring even amidst the chaos. He leaned in, his lips brushing my ear as he whispered, "I'm here. I'll stay with you through every moment of this, Jemima. You're not alone. We're in this together."

His words pierced through the haze of pain, his presence easing the panic that had begun to claw at me. I focused on him—on the warmth of his touch, the strength in his voice. It was like a lifeline, an anchor in the storm of pain that raged within me.

But the contractions kept coming, each one fiercer, more demanding than the last. My legs cramped as I tried to brace myself against the jolting of the carriage, my body fighting against itself. I tried to push, desperate to end this agony, but nothing happened. The pressure remained, my belly still hard as a stone, the babies refusing to budge no matter how hard I tried.

Frustration boiled within me, mixing with the pain until I was sobbing against Josiah's shoulder, my breaths ragged and desperate. "They won't... they won't move," I managed to say, my voice breaking. "It feels like—like they're stuck."

He pulled me closer, his hand smoothing over my hair, his touch a steady comfort amidst the chaos. "It's all right," he murmured, his thumb tracing gentle circles against my hand. "Just breathe, one moment at a time. We'll get through this, Jemima. I promise you."

I nodded, tears spilling down my cheeks, trying to draw strength from his words. There was something in his gaze, a vulnerability I hadn't noticed before, and it steadied me, his strength and gentleness giving me something to cling to when everything else felt like it was slipping away.

Another contraction subsided, leaving me panting for breath, my body trembling from the strain. As I leaned back, trying to find some small reprieve, Josiah looked at me, his expression softening. His eyes were filled with something that made my heart twist—a sorrow, an unspoken weight that he had carried alone.

"Jemima," he began, his voice low and thick. He swallowed, his eyes never leaving mine. "Are you okay? Is the pain too much?"

I blinked, trying to focus through the fog of pain, nodding slightly, though my breath hitched with each contraction. He continued, his voice filled with concern.

"Why do you have to go through this?" he whispered, his voice filled with an emotion I couldn't quite place. "Is there anything I can do to help?"

I tried to speak through the pain, my breath hitching as I managed to look at him. "Just... stay with me," I whispered, my voice cracking. "That's all I need, Josiah."

Another contraction ripped through me before I could respond, my body arching as I cried out, my hands clutching at his coat. The pain was all-consuming, drowning out everything else. He leaned in, his forehead resting gently against mine, his breath warm against my skin. "I'm so sorry, Jemima," he whispered, his voice breaking. "I made you go through all this alone."

I shook my head, tears streaming down my face as I gasped for breath. "No," I managed, my voice trembling. "No, I'm happy to have given birth to our baby, Josiah."

His eyes shimmered with unshed tears, and he kissed my forehead, his lips lingering there as if to seal the moment. "Thank you," he said quietly, his voice thick with emotion.

The pain eased slightly, just enough for me to catch my breath, and I looked up at him, my heart swelling with a warmth that seemed to push back the shadows that had clouded it for so long. Despite everything—despite the anger, the bitterness that had once held me captive—I trusted him now. He had shown me a care that went beyond duty, a loyalty that was deeper than obligation, and I could feel my heart softening, opening to him in a way I hadn't allowed before.

"Thank you," I whispered, my voice trembling with emotion. "For being here. For... everything."

He nodded, his gaze unwavering as he brushed a tear from my cheek, his hand lingering on my face, his touch filled with a tenderness that made my heart ache. "You don't need to thank me, Jemima. I'm right where I want to be. With you."

Another contraction struck, fiercer than the last, and I cried out, clutching his hand as the pain wracked through me. My body trembled, my muscles straining, but this time, with him by my side, his voice in my ear, his hand steady in mine, I felt a strength I hadn't known before. I could do this. I would do this—with him.

The storm continued to rage outside, the rain pounding against the carriage, the wind howling through the trees. But here, inside this small, swaying box, Josiah was my world. I leaned into him, letting his presence steady me, his words guide me through the pain. Each wave became more bearable, more endurable with his gentle reassurances, his unwavering belief in me.

And in that moment, I knew—whatever the future held, whatever challenges lay ahead, we would face them together, bound by something far stronger than duty. Something that, in the midst of this pain and vulnerability, felt a great deal like love.

40

The Futile Effort

The carriage jolted with each gust of wind, and I held Jemima's hand tightly, feeling the strain of her grip as she fought through each wave of pain. She leaned back, her body trembling with exhaustion, her face pale and glistening with sweat. Each contraction seemed worse than the last, sharper, stronger, more unforgiving. Her breaths came in shallow gasps, her chest heaving as she tried to find some relief. But there was no relief, only the constant, overwhelming pain.

She had tried everything—sitting upright, leaning forward, even lying down when the pain grew too intense—but nothing seemed to work. She shifted positions again and again, trying to ease the unbearable pressure, her face twisted in agony as she desperately sought some relief. Every movement seemed to intensify the pain rather than soothe it, and her breaths grew more labored, her body drenched in sweat as each contraction came faster and harder, leaving her exhausted and defeated. The cramped carriage left her with no space to move, no space to find comfort, every lurch sending another ripple of agony through her belly and spine. Her rounded stomach, once a source of joy and anticipation, now felt like a prison, stretched taut, the babies inside refusing to budge despite her every effort.

"Josiah—" she gasped, her voice raw, her hand squeezing mine with a desperation that tore at my heart. "Please—look... I need you to look and see if... if you can see them..."

I swallowed hard, my heart hammering in my chest. I knelt down as best I could in the small space, doing as she asked, praying desperately to see some sign that her struggle wasn't in vain. I peered through the dim light that filtered in through the rain-streaked windows, searching, hoping. But there was nothing—only the unyielding barrier of her body, her pain without visible progress. It was as though the babies were determined to stay sheltered within her, despite her agony.

I looked up at her, my throat tight, shaking my head as regret filled my voice. "Nothing, Jemima. I'm sorry... I don't see anything yet."

She let out a cry, a raw, broken sound, her frustration mingling with the unending pain. Her hands clawed at the carriage walls, her back arching as another contraction tore through her. Her face twisted in agony, her body tensing as she tried to push, her swollen belly tightening with a force that seemed almost unbearable.

I reached out, gently guiding her back, my hands on her shoulders, my heart aching with every cry she let out. "You're doing so well, Jemima," I whispered, my voice trembling despite my attempts to stay calm. "Just breathe, take it one moment at a time."

But she shook her head, her eyes wild, tears streaming down her face as she fought to find some relief. "It hurts—oh, God, it hurts so much—" she sobbed, her hands pressing against her belly as though she could force the babies out by sheer will alone. Her nails dug into the fabric of her dress, her body shaking with the effort.

I pulled her into my arms, holding her close, my hand stroking her hair as she trembled against me. "I'm here, Jemima," I whispered, my voice cracking as I tried to stay strong for her. "We'll get through this. Just hold on a little longer."

She sobbed against my chest, her fingers clutching at my coat, her body shaking with the force of her pain. I felt utterly helpless, unable to do anything but hold her, whispering words of comfort that felt so small in the face of what she was enduring.

"Josiah," she whimpered, her voice barely audible, filled with a vulnerability that made my heart ache. "I don't think I can... I can't do this. They won't… they won't come."

"You can do this, Jemima," I replied, my voice as steady as I could manage, though inside I felt like I was breaking. "You're the strongest person I know. Just hold on a little longer. We're going to get through this together."

She looked at me, her eyes filled with despair, her body slumping against the seat as she gasped for breath, the fight seeming to leave her. The storm outside was relentless, the rain pounding against the carriage, the wind howling, and I knew she was reaching her limit.

I took her hand, pressing it to my chest, hoping she could feel the steady beat of my heart, the quiet assurance that she wasn't alone. "I'm here, Jemima," I murmured, leaning close, my forehead resting against hers. "I'm not leaving you. Not now, not ever."

She looked at me, her gaze softening, a flicker of trust passing between us even as the pain returned, fierce and unyielding. Her back arched, her hands clutching at the seat as she let out another scream, her entire body straining with the effort.

"Please… Josiah… help me. I can't… I can't do it alone," she cried, her voice breaking as her fingers dug into my arm.

I held her as tightly as I dared, my hand at the small of her back, supporting her. "You're not alone, Jemima," I whispered, my voice thick with emotion. "I'm with you. And I'll stay with you until they're here, until this is over. Just hold on a little longer."

She nodded, her face streaked with tears, her breaths coming in shallow gasps as she braced herself for the next wave. And as I watched her, as I felt the weight of her trust in me, I knew that my life, my heart, belonged to her entirely.

The storm raged on, unrelenting, the wind and rain battering the world outside. But here, in this small, confined space, I felt a quiet strength blossom between us—a fragile hope that bound us together, even in the face of this agony, this pain.

No matter what happened, no matter what the future held, I would remain by her side. Her protector, her partner, her husband in every sense of the word.

41

The Birth

The carriage rocked violently with each gust of wind, and I held Jemima's hand tightly, feeling the force of her grip as she fought through each wave of agonizing pain. Her other hand clutched her swollen belly tightly, her fingers pressing into the taut skin as if trying to steady the life within her, to anchor herself amidst the storm and the pain.

I barely registered the sound of the carriage door opening, the rough footsteps splashing through the mud as the driver returned, drenched and breathless. His voice was muffled, distorted by the storm and my own labored breathing, but then another voice joined his—gentle, soothing, yet firm. A woman's voice. Relief surged through me, sharp and unexpected, as the village midwife climbed into the cramped space, her calm, knowing eyes immediately assessing the situation.

"Your Grace," she murmured, nodding to me before turning her full attention to Jemima. Her hands were warm and steady as she laid them on Jemima's belly, her voice a balm against the chaos of pain and panic that had overtaken us. "You've done so well, my dear. We're nearly there now. Let us bring these little ones into the world."

Exhaustion weighed heavily on Jemima, her strength waning with each contraction, her body trembling from the relentless effort. I could see her face, pale and glistening with sweat, her eyes clouded with pain. She was worn, so utterly drained, yet she clung to the midwife's words, to the certainty that this ordeal would soon come to an end. I knelt beside her, my hand still in hers, holding on as tightly as I could, my gaze fixed upon her face, filled with concern and a fierce determination to be by her side. I willed her to feel my love, my unwavering strength, and let it carry her through the storm.

"Jemima," I murmured, leaning closer, my voice filled with emotion that I had kept hidden for too long. "I'm here. You're not alone. I'm right here with you."

She nodded, her lips trembling, tears spilling down her cheeks, mingling with the sweat that dampened her brow. I could see how deeply the fatigue had set in, her breaths coming in shallow, desperate gasps. But with my hand in hers, with the midwife's steady guidance, there was a glimmer of hope, a faint belief that she could do this—that we could do this together.

The midwife's instructions were clear and gentle, her voice guiding Jemima through each contraction. She positioned herself to assist, her hands ready, her words a lifeline as Jemima struggled to breathe, to push, to bring our children into the world. I could feel Jemima's grip on my hand tighten with every wave, her strength seeming to ebb and flow like the tide. Her cries were raw, agonized, and my heart broke with each one, wishing that I could take her pain upon myself.

"You're doing wonderfully, Jemima," I whispered, my forehead resting against hers as she fought through each wave, my breath steadying hers as I tried to be her anchor. "Just a little longer, my love. You are so close."

Time became a blur, each contraction merging into the next, every push an act of sheer willpower as her body strained, her heart pounding with desperation. Her belly tightened fiercely with each wave, the babies shifting within, her skin taut and stretched as though it could barely contain them. The movements of the babies were almost visible, a reminder of how close we were, yet so far. Her cries of pain were matched only by the fierce determination in her eyes, a refusal to give in to the agony that racked her body. And then, finally, a moment of release—a moment so profound that it left me breathless—as the first baby entered the world, his cries piercing through the howling storm outside.

"A boy," the midwife announced, her voice warm with pride as she handed him to Jemima, his tiny, wriggling form nestled against her chest. My heart swelled, my breath catching as I looked down at him—red and wrinkled, his cries loud and full of life. I felt tears sting my eyes, a deep sense of awe washing over me as I wrapped an arm around Jemima, my face close to hers as I gazed at our son.

But there was no time to rest. The midwife quickly prepared Jemima for the next birth, her voice firm but kind as she encouraged her to keep going. Jemima was exhausted, her body trembling, her strength all but gone. Her belly, once tight and swollen with the weight of both children, now shifted visibly as the second baby moved lower, her abdomen contracting painfully. The size of her belly had diminished slightly after the first birth, but it still held a taut roundness, each movement of the second baby causing her to wince. I could see it in her eyes, the weariness, the doubt, but the sight of our son, his small hand grasping weakly at her finger, filled her with a strength she hadn't known she possessed.

"Just a little more, Jemima," I murmured, my hand brushing a damp strand of hair from her face, my voice steady, though my heart ached for her. "You are almost there. One more, my love."

With a final, desperate push, Jemima let out a cry that seemed to echo through the very storm itself, her body arching with the effort. And then, the second baby entered the world, her cries joining her brother's, filling the small, dimly lit space of the carriage with a sound so pure, so fierce, that it brought tears to my eyes. The midwife wrapped her gently, her smile soft as she placed her in Jemima's arms beside her brother.

"A girl," she said, her voice tinged with warmth and pride. "You have a son and a daughter, Your Grace."

Jemima looked down at our children, their tiny bodies nestled against her, their cries softening as they settled into her embrace. They were perfect, each one a tiny miracle that seemed to hold the weight of the world within them. I could barely breathe, the exhaustion mingling with a profound, aching joy that filled me completely.

I leaned closer, my hand resting over Jemima's as I gazed down at them, my heart full to bursting. "They are beautiful, Jemima," I whispered, my voice thick with emotion. "Just like their mother."

Jemima looked up at me, her eyes glistening with tears, her lips curving into a weary smile. In that moment, I truly saw her—not as the woman burdened by duty, not as the figure of obligation I had once thought her to be, but as my partner, my beloved, the mother of my children, the woman who had fought through so much and come out stronger on the other side.

"Thank you, Josiah," she whispered, her voice barely audible, but I heard every word, felt the weight of her gratitude. "For everything."

I shook my head, my own tears falling freely as I brushed a gentle kiss against her forehead. "No, Jemima," I replied, my voice filled with quiet reverence. "Thank you. You have given me everything I never dared to dream of."

We sat there together, the storm still raging outside, but within the carriage, there was only warmth, only love. I felt the weight of my children in my arms, the gentle strength of Jemima beside me, and for the first time, I felt truly at peace.

As I looked down at my son and daughter, nestled close, I knew that whatever challenges lay ahead, whatever trials we would face, we would do it together—bound by the love that had grown between us, by the family we had created in the midst of the storm.

And in that moment, I felt a hope, a joy that went beyond words—a future that was ours to shape, to nurture, to cherish.

42

A Love Beyond Duty

The storm had finally passed, leaving a profound silence in its wake, the rain's patter softened to a gentle hum against the carriage roof. In that stillness, I sat quietly, gazing down at the tiny, swaddled figure cradled in my arms—our son. He was impossibly small, his fingers barely brushing mine as I traced the delicate curve of his hand, his face serene, as though he had brought the calm with him. A peaceful warmth settled over me, wrapping itself around my heart and filling it in a way that nothing ever had.

A pang rose in my chest, something fierce and tender all at once. A love that had taken root deep inside me, unexpected and overwhelming, filling spaces I hadn't known were empty. This was my son. And my daughter—our children, born out of a journey that had taken us from cold duty to something beautiful and irrevocable.

Beside me, Jemima cradled our daughter, her face illuminated by the soft light filtering through the rain-streaked windows, her expression softened in a way that made my breath catch. She looked radiant, her beauty heightened by the tender glow of motherhood. As she gazed down at the sleeping infant in her arms, I could see a kind of love there that went beyond words—a raw, protective fierceness that spoke of her devotion to the two lives we had brought into the world. When she looked up, her eyes met mine, and in them, I saw warmth—a warmth I had never dared to hope for, a warmth that spoke of acceptance and perhaps, finally, of love.

Without thinking, I reached out, my fingers brushing hers as our children lay between us, a bridge that bound us together more deeply than any words ever could. I marveled at the sight of our hands, joined as they rested over the little bundles, our children nestled between us.

"Jemima," I murmured, my voice thick with emotion, "I don't think I can ever thank you enough... for bringing them into our lives." My eyes held hers, my heart swelling with a depth of feeling I found difficult to contain.

She looked down at our daughter, then back at me, her lips curving into the gentlest of smiles, her eyes misting slightly. "I never expected this... any of it," she admitted, her voice soft, barely a whisper. "But I'm... grateful. More grateful than I ever thought I could be." Her gaze held mine, and in it, I saw everything—every hurt, every fear, every moment that had brought us here. The tension and distrust that had once shadowed her eyes were gone, replaced by something far gentler. It was as if the storm had stripped away all the resentment, all the fears, leaving us raw, open to the possibility of something new.

My heart swelled at her words, my fingers tightening around hers. I leaned closer, my thumb gently brushing her knuckles. "I never expected this either," I confessed, my voice barely louder than the soft rustle of rain against the carriage. "But, Jemima... you've made me realize what love truly is. I want you to know, from this day forward, I'm here. Not out of duty, not out of obligation—but because I love you."

Her eyes glistened, a tear slipping down her cheek as she smiled, a smile that reached her very soul. She turned slightly, her daughter still cradled to her chest, and looked at me with a tenderness that made my breath catch. "Josiah," she whispered, her voice trembling. "I... I love you too. More than I ever thought possible."

Her words hung between us, simple and true, a testament to the journey we had taken, the obstacles we had overcome, and the love that had blossomed in the unlikeliest of places. We had come together out of duty, out of a sense of honor and responsibility, but somewhere along the way, those bonds had transformed, deepened, until they had become something precious and irreplaceable.

I reached out, cupping her cheek, my thumb brushing away the tear that lingered there. Then I leaned in, pressing my lips softly to hers—a kiss that was gentle, filled with reverence, and yet holding within it every promise that words could never fully convey. She kissed me back, her lips warm and soft, and I felt the world fall away—there was no storm, no darkness, only this moment, only us. When we pulled apart, I rested my forehead against hers, our breaths mingling, our hearts beating as one.

"Look at them," Jemima whispered, her gaze dropping to the tiny bundles between us. "They're perfect." Her voice was filled with wonder, her eyes tracing every tiny feature of our son and daughter, the softness of their cheeks, the gentle rise and fall of their breathing.

"They are," I agreed, my own gaze fixed on our children. "And so are you." My voice caught, my throat tightening as I took in the sight of my wife, our children—our family. This was everything I had never dared to dream of, everything I hadn't known I needed until now.

Jemima looked back at me, her eyes full of love, and then asked, "Have you thought of names for them, Josiah?"

I smiled, nodding softly as I reached out, my hand resting gently on our son's tiny chest. "For our son, I thought of Jasper," I said, my voice tender. "It means 'bringer of treasure.' And that's what he is—a treasure, a blessing we never expected."

Jemima's eyes softened, and she nodded, her gaze dropping lovingly to our son. "Jasper," she murmured, testing the name. "It's perfect."

I then shifted my gaze to our daughter, cradled so lovingly in Jemima's arms. "And for our daughter, I thought of Juliet," I said, my voice almost a whisper. "It means 'youthful' and 'full of energy.' She's our little light, bringing hope and joy."

Jemima's smile widened, her eyes misting again as she looked at our daughter. "Juliet," she repeated softly, her voice filled with wonder. "It's beautiful."

We sat together, our children cradled between us, the storm now a distant memory. In the wake of that tempest, we had found each other, stripped of all pretense and guardedness. We had found love—a love that surpassed duty, transcending titles and expectations, a love that was pure and true.

I knew, deep in my heart, that whatever lay ahead, we would face it together. Jemima was no longer just my wife—she was my partner, my equal, and the love of my life. And as we held our children close, I knew that this was the beginning of something beautiful, a future we would shape, nurture, and cherish—together.

43

Love Refined

The days had grown warmer, the fields around the manor lush and green, and the air filled with the soft hum of springtime. I sat by the nursery window, gazing out at the vibrant landscape, my daughter nestled in my arms, her tiny hand grasping my finger with an innocence that still took my breath away. Beside her crib, our son stirred, his gentle coos filling the room with a sweetness that made me smile.

Months had passed since that stormy night, since the intensity of labor, the rawness of pain, and the sheer vulnerability that had laid us bare to one another. Life had shifted since then, falling into a rhythm I had once doubted we'd ever find. But here we were, building a life together—not out of obligation or duty, but out of a love that had grown steadily, quietly, resilient as wildflowers pushing up through stone.

The warmth of the spring sun touched my skin, and I felt an overwhelming sense of peace, a peace that had once seemed impossible. For so long, I had been locked in a prison of my own making—of resentment, of suspicion, of fear. I had carried Simon's memory with me, wearing it like a shield against vulnerability. I'd thought that by clinging to the past, by holding on to the image of the life I'd imagined with him, I was protecting myself from the pain of the present.

Simon. My heart no longer twisted with bitterness at the thought of his name, but there was still a lingering ache—a gentle sadness for what could never be. I had once loved him with the fervor of youth, blind to his flaws, blind to the burdens he had placed upon others, especially upon Josiah. In my grief, I had painted Josiah in the same hues, refusing to see him for who he truly was. I had been so convinced that he was nothing more than a replacement, a poor shadow of Simon, and I had treated him as such.

A soft knock at the door stirred me from my reverie. I looked up to see Josiah standing in the doorway, his eyes warm as he watched me, a gentle smile playing at his lips.

"Jemima," he murmured, crossing the room to stand beside me, his gaze drifting from me to our daughter. "How are they?"

"Perfect," I replied softly, a sense of peace settling over me. I still marveled at the tenderness in his gaze, the quiet strength he showed in the small gestures—a hand on my back, a gentle brush of my hair, an understanding that went unspoken yet felt deeply.

He leaned down, pressing a kiss to our daughter's head before straightening and looking back at me, his hand resting on my shoulder. "And you, my love?" he asked, his tone filled with genuine care. "Are you happy?"

I looked up at him, feeling a rush of warmth, a gratitude that went beyond words. I had spent so long locked in bitterness, in suspicion, building walls to keep myself safe. Yet he had broken down those walls, not with force, but with gentleness, with a patience that had allowed me to rediscover trust, to find joy in a life I hadn't thought possible.

"Yes," I replied, my voice barely a whisper. "I am, Josiah. More than I ever thought I could be."

We stood together in comfortable silence, watching our children, and I felt a bond between us that was more than just affection or respect. It was a unity forged through trial, through a willingness to understand each other's deepest wounds, to let go of old fears and embrace the unknown.

I remembered the way I had once looked at him, my eyes clouded with judgment, refusing to see the man beneath the title. I had been so certain that he could never truly care for me, that he was merely fulfilling a duty. I had pushed him away, hurt him with my mistrust, and yet he had stayed—patient, unwavering. He had borne the burden of Simon's sins, shouldered the weight of my resentment, and still, he had offered me kindness. I realized now how wrong I had been, how unfairly I had treated him. And yet, he had forgiven me without question, had loved me even when I could not love myself.

When we ventured into society these days, it was different than before. The scandal that had once haunted Josiah had all but faded, the whispers and rumors losing their power in the face of the life we had created. We faced the world side by side, his hand in mine, each glance, each smile shared between us a quiet testament to the journey we had taken.

People still watched us, curious and sometimes awed, perhaps seeing in us a partnership they hadn't expected. I could see it in their eyes—a mix of surprise and admiration, as though they, too, were witnessing the transformation that had unfolded.

Josiah, my once-stranger husband, was now my partner in every sense, my confidant, my dearest friend. I had come to know his heart, his unwavering loyalty, his quiet courage, and I cherished each of these things as treasures beyond measure. He had once been the man bound by duty, by a weight not his own, but now he was free—we were free—to live by our own terms, together.

"Do you remember," he said, breaking the silence, his voice tinged with a lightness I'd come to adore, "when you first accepted this marriage?" He chuckled, a mischievous spark in his eyes. "You looked as if you might run from me at any moment."

I laughed, a blush rising to my cheeks as I looked away. "Yes, I remember. I had... my doubts." I glanced up at him, a small smile tugging at my lips. "I suppose I didn't make it easy for you."

"No," he replied, smiling back with a gentleness that made my heart swell. "But I wouldn't change a thing. It led us here, to this life, to... us."

His hand found mine, our fingers intertwining, and I felt a surge of gratitude so deep it made my breath catch. Together, we had built something true, something lasting, far beyond the boundaries of duty or obligation. It was a love refined by fire, resilient and enduring, the kind that could weather any storm.

As the sun set, casting a warm glow over the nursery, I looked at him, knowing with absolute certainty that this was the life I wanted, the love

I would cherish forever. Whatever lay ahead, we would face it together, stronger, unwavering, and deeply, irrevocably bound to one another.

Josiah leaned closer, his eyes searching mine, and I could see the love reflected in his gaze—a love that had grown through all the challenges we had faced. Slowly, he cupped my cheek with his hand, his thumb gently brushing my skin, and I felt a warmth spread through me.

"I don't think I'll ever stop loving you. I'm eternally yours," he whispered, his voice soft and filled with emotion. "I love you, Jemima."

Tears welled in my eyes as I smiled, my heart swelling with a happiness I could scarcely contain. "And I love you, Josiah," I replied, my voice trembling with the depth of my feelings.

He leaned in, and our lips met in a gentle, tender kiss, a kiss that spoke of promises made and kept, of hope and love and a future we would build together. It was a kiss that sealed everything we had endured and everything we had become—a kiss that bound us in a way that words never could.

When we finally pulled apart, I rested my forehead against his, our breaths mingling, and I knew that this was home—here, in his arms, surrounded by our children and the love we had fought so hard to nurture.

* * *

As the delicate strains of the season's final ball fade into the night, a dark mystery looms over London's nobility: the young and beautiful new Duchess of Wakefield is widowed, pregnant, and facing a ruthless society that questions her every move.

Forced to marry the ailing Duke to settle her family's debts, Lady Evelina never expected her life to spiral into scandal. When the Duke's sudden passing leaves her future—and the future of her unborn child—in jeopardy, whispers of doubt swirl among the ton. Her only ally? A captivating, battle-worn gentleman who appears on the Duke's orders, ready to stand by Evelina through the trials that await her.

But as society's judgment closes in, Evelina and her newfound protector must unravel the secrets her husband left behind. Can they secure her child's legacy…or will her mysterious defender spark a scandal greater than any the ton has ever known?

THE DUKE'S INHERITED BRIDE

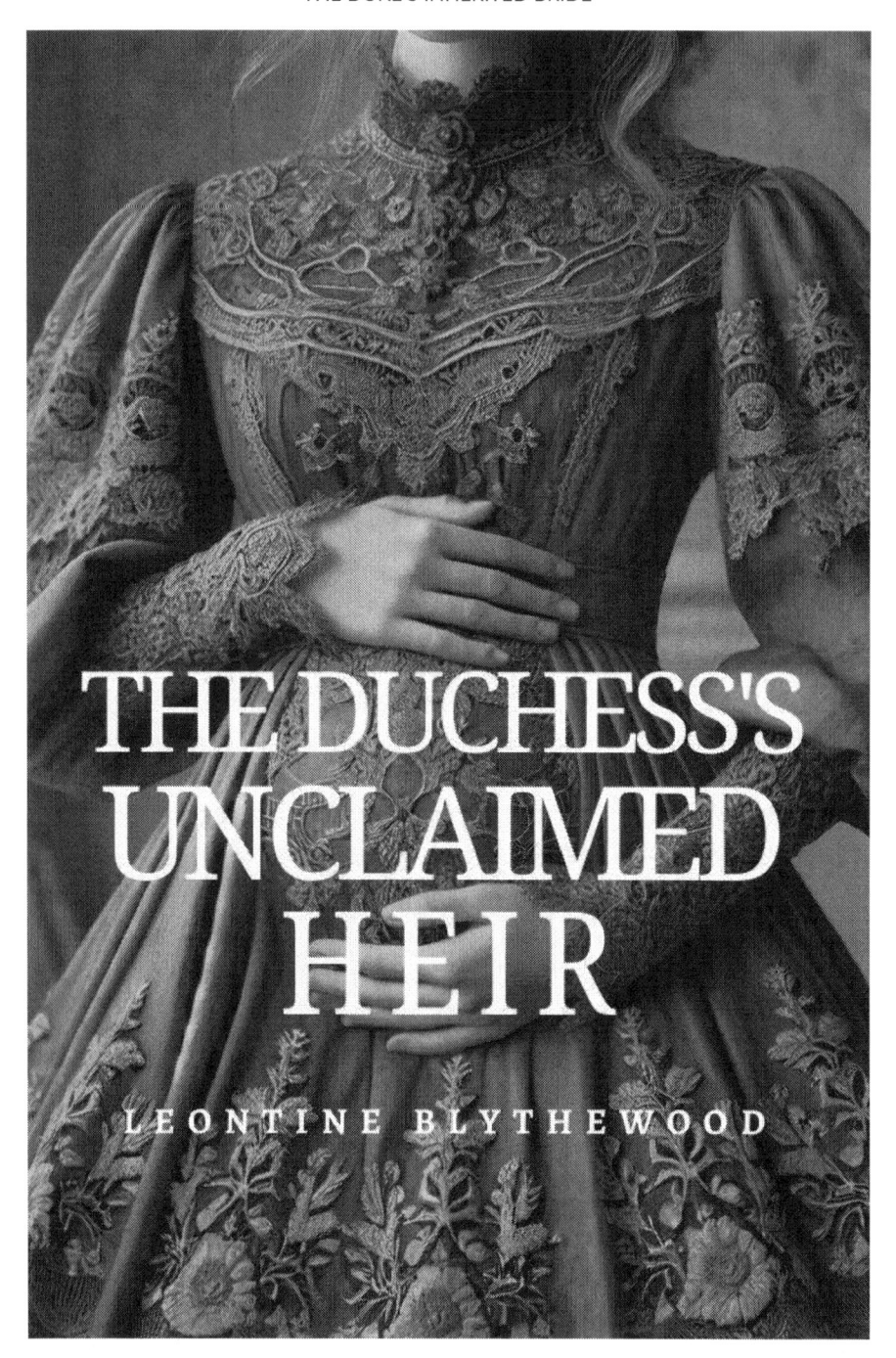

THE DUCHESS'S UNCLAIMED HEIR

LEONTINE BLYTHEWOOD

About the Author

Leontine Blythewood is a Regency romance writer who revels in scandal, intrigue, and the thrill of conflict. She likes to create tales of stolen glances, whispered secrets, and the razor's edge of propriety. She also wants her stories to leave readers wondering who will emerge unscathed-or delightfully ruined.

Beyond the drama of her novels, Leontine lives a quieter life. An avowed feline devotee, she finds inspiration in her feline companions' unpredictable natures and unmistakable disdain for society's rules.

Printed in Great Britain
by Amazon